One Dream

&

Collected Stories

One Dream

&

Collected Stories

a novel by
Bet Shoshannah Pecora
& stories by anonymous

Published
by
Polar Bear & Company
Solon, Maine U.S.A.
www.polarbearandco.com

The opinions, findings, and conclusions or recommendations expressed in this publication are those of the authors and do not necessarily reflect the views of the Department of Justice, the Maine Office of Substance Abuse (DMHMRSAS), or AdCare Educational Institute.

Funding for the printing of this book was provided exclusively by Polar Bear & Co.

Polar Bear & Company
P.O. Box 311, Solon, Maine 04979 U.S.A.
207 643-2795
polarbear@skow.net

For more information and tales to read with new ideas visit www.polarbearandco.com, where the theme is:
Mythology for modern democracy brings variety to everyday life!

First edition. Manufactured with soy based ink on recycled paper in the U.S.A. by Thomson - Shore, Inc.
ISBN 1-882190-60-2

Contents

From Governor Angus King of Maine

I was fortunate enough to grow up in a simpler age. Days were spent playing sandlot ball, curled away in the corner of the library, or fishing with my dad. Today, though, the pressures facing young people are enormous - substance abuse, violence, demands to succeed, one-parent households, to name just a few. It's hard to imagine the stress this must induce.

Our society is pretty good at producing data - we can tell you how many children have parents who drink, or how many end up abusing alcohol themselves - but sociologists can't peer into the human soul. This is the magical thing about this book - it tells these stories, and how our kids survive them - in their own words. By writing about their experiences with alcohol abuse, *One Dream and Collected Stories* will help us all to understand the real-life impact of substance abuse.

Whether it's Bet Pecora's novel or the personal stories collected through Youth Voices, there is a message here for us all: that our children are growing up faster, that they need our help, and that hope and love can still work miracles.

Thank you for listening to these children. Their voices are compelling, but ultimately reassuring.

Angus S. King, Jr.
Governor

Foreword

In the late summer and autumn, here in Central Maine, as in other places, we can pick wild berries and apples for pies; you will also find that some of the apples get pressed in homemade cider presses to go down into basements where they ferment into a delicious hard cider, mixed perhaps with maple syrup, to last until the apples return. Idyllic memories of Maine's lakes, rivers and forests, of the harvest in the vegetable garden, of pumpkins, of salmon on the barbecue, where alcohol is not so much an issue as a fermented food blended with the changes of the seasons, are possible when we know that they inhabit the same world with the same dreams as the one described in this book.

Sometimes it can be nearly impossible to see the connection. Under pressure of such heavy issues it's not unusual to respond with the cliché, "What's it got to do with me?" Without novels and stories like this to look into the personal relationships, it can be difficult to see how the same social pressures that lead to substance abuse can filter round to seemingly unrelated circumstances, such as the environment, for example, and cloud our decisions and then our dreams in areas where addiction does not seem to be a factor.

For a guest to refer to the aforementioned cider as a "substance" could be anti-social; to abuse it, even more so! To say this in the context of this book is possibly a bit alarming. But as we know, different regions have different customs. Many other countries don't have the same degree of trouble with alcohol and drugs as we do in the States; but maybe they don't have many of the social pressures a leading democracy like ours has, where breakthroughs in freedom are expected, sometimes dreaded, which is anything but an excuse or a way to pass the buck. Surely many of the answers to social pressure lie in the communication represented by this book and in many kinds of cross cultural exchanges, regional and generational. And surely one of the ongoing lessons of the prohibition era is that it's important to develop a climate where we feel we can express ourselves democratically, to find that creative balance in many areas of life, including food and drink, and drug legislation.

Serious issues are often hard to deal with in casual everyday conversations. We turn to the news, movies, TV, music and the written word to help us understand our society. It's hard to filter all the information and seek out the truth. We have been lucky to come across a book that highlights topics we all need to discuss. A novel that uncovers the roots to questions that need answering, while entertaining. A book that speaks honestly about the pressures in society that make us act in ways that are contrary to how we envisaged ourselves being. A book that gives direction and hope. *One Dream and Collected Stories* is such a book.

Our goal as a publisher has been to give youth a place for their voices in print. We simply wish for you to read what they sometimes have to endure, to see life through their eyes.

It has taken a great deal of courage for these young leaders to come forth with these stories. We are fortunate to have the opportunity of working with Youth Voices and Bet Shoshannah Pecora. It gives us hope that the future will be brighter with the spirit, enthusiasm and love these young adults have.

Polar Bear & Company

Introduction

What is so powerful about the voices of today's youth? Could it be that they are rarely heard - that young people are so often put into the role of listener and student that a serious medium through which they can express themselves is almost nonexistent?

Here is a book that provides insight into the world of today's youth - a generation searching for the truth in the midst of pop culture and mass media - a generation with access to more information and technology than anyone preceding them. What have these young, bright faces to which the media, parents and teachers preach, often not listening for a response, done with all of the information piled upon them?

Here is the answer on the controversial issue of substance abuse. What does this generation think about underage drinking? What are the situations that these individuals experience that they avoid discussing with the adults in their lives? Drugs are a difficult topic to tackle, thus they are often avoided in conversation - especially in dialogue between adults and adolescents. What, then, is the truth about substance abuse and teenagers?

There are laws in place to regulate alcohol consumption, and keep it out of the hands of minors. How much respect do these laws hold when advertising campaigns portray young, attractive people having fun while drinking, or cartoon characters cracking jokes about alcohol? If it is adults who create these advertisements, is it the youth who have a problem with underage drinking?

Young people frequently feel frustrated with listening to lectures about alcohol. Adults feel the frustration of their passionate lectures falling upon deaf ears. Maybe, instead of taking the role of "educator," adults should practice listening a little more. More important, after listening, maybe they should reevaluate the often mixed messages that they are sending to the youth about whom they care deeply.

To the adult readers: Here is your chance to listen to the answers to these essential questions. While reading, please understand that the youth do no want to place blame. They simply want to communicate with you.

To the young readers: The hope is that you will find what you are looking for in these pages. The inspiration to use your voice, and the determination to find creative ways to make others listen.

Kate Drummond
Youth Voices Adult Coordinator

One Dream

a novel by
Bet Shoshannah Pecora

Dedication

All my dedications and thanks to Jamie Thomas and Mrs. Sears. If it were not for them, I would never have finished this book successfully.

Bet Shoshannah Pecora

Prologue

Even after all this time, I still love to watch the stars. Sitting on the stoop and staring up at the night sky seemed harder then, thinking about nothing... but everything. I think I'm dreaming when I remember my mom telling me stories about when I was a child, how I'd fall asleep every night just looking at the stars. She would have to carry me in and put me to bed. That was when she was normal, not a drunk.

That was so long ago, and I don't know why I try to remember it. For some reason, thinking of those times seems important to me. Remembering the bad things makes me a little stronger every day, and the good make me happy. When I realize how far I've gone, I feel proud of myself, and I'm shocked.

The stars were really all I had. You may think me weird, but it is true. My dad ran out on my mom when he found out she was pregnant. It was a one night stand with a sweet and beautiful, easy, high school girl. She was only in the eleventh grade when she gave birth. She had to drop out of high school because of me. I guess that is why she stressed my education, and to stay away from girls.

My mom never had a great childhood. Maybe that is why she didn't know how to handle me. My mom always said her parents never loved her. She was an only child and mostly raised by the maids. Her parents were always on business trips and never had time for their child.

When my mom told my grandma that she was pregnant, my grandma totally flipped out. Her father and mother did not talk to her at all. One day my mom asked for their forgiveness.

They had a big argument, and my grandparents told my mom they raised their daughter better than that. My mom told them they did not raise her at all, the maids did. They kicked her out. Sometimes I think my mom wanted to get pregnant, just so her parents would notice her.

My mom moved in with a friend who was kicked out of her house because of drugs. They shared a cheap apartment in a building that was falling apart. She found a job at a fast-food restaurant, but soon was fired for being rude to the customers. She looked around awhile for a new job, but could not find anything. Her friend kicked us out because my mom could not pay rent. I was five then.

We lived out on the streets for about a year. On my sixth birthday we went to a shelter. That was when my mom started drinking. She said the world was at an end when a well-to-do girl had to live in a shelter, with a six-year-old son.

No one would hire my mom. After all, who wants a drunk who is undependable and late every day? One man at the shelter found my mom one of those jobs they give to homeless people. It was just a simple job at a cat food factory, and it was low pay, but it was work. The people at her new job said they hired people off the street because they "wanted to give them a good turn in life." My mom didn't like that quote that much.

When I was eight, my mom had enough money to rent a one room apartment. We lived there until I was sixteen. It was really shaggy, with hardly any furniture. When I looked at the green couch with the stuffing coming out, or the tattered curtains, or the torn rug, I just thanked God at least we had heat and a roof over our heads. I was glad to live in a "home" for once, even if it was trashy.

I was sixteen when my life took a turn for the worse. I was just like all the other teenagers of the world, fighting with problems like drugs, school, and just making it through life. Almost every night I sat on my stoop, leaned back, and stared at the stars. I thought about when I was younger, and tried to imagine what my father was like. I also tried to conquer fear. Fear of not fitting in, fear of life, fear of my mother.

My friends always teased me for staring at the stars. I lived in the city, and had really tough friends. They seemed to understand a little, or maybe they just didn't care. Whenever another gang came and asked why I liked the stars, my friends would tell them that I was from the planet, Jupiter, where there were no stars. And I was so fascinated with the always new found miracle that I couldn't keep my eyes away. It was humiliating, but they were just trying to help me from not being beat up for being a dork.

I don't care what they say, I love the stars. They don't yell, throw things, hit, or offer drugs. They almost, understand. Their only job is to twinkle and be beautiful. After all, they helped me to fulfill my dream.

Chapter 1

“Hey, Joe! Wait up!" My best friend, Adam Smith, always called me Joe, even though that is not my name. For some reason he thought it was funny. It was just really annoying. "Hey, what's your hurry? What you trying to do, run all the way to the Olympics 2004?" he asked, while catching up to me.

"Going to be late for class. Woke up late this morning," I said, still walking fast. "I can't afford any more tardies."

"What you do, fall asleep watching the stars?" Adam always teased me about the stars, but somehow I knew that he knew where I was coming from. It was not just a habit or pastime, staring at the stars. But more of an escape from the world, much better than drugs.

"Not really. I got thrown out again," I snapped back and gave him an evil look. He should watch what he says, even if I do know he is kidding around.

"What happened this time, did you cook her dinner and she didn't like what you made?" Adam ignored my snap. He was the one and only person who knew about my mom. I was ashamed of telling anybody else. Most of my friends had worse homes than me, like a father that smacks them around.

"No, I was talking to Suzy on the phone when she came home. You know how she gets when I talk to girls. Well, she took the phone, tore it out of the wall, and threw it at me. She forbade me to see, talk, or converse with Suzy anymore. She told me to get out, so I slept on the street last night." I shrugged when I said that last sentence. It happened a lot, being kicked out. It didn't really bother me much anymore, almost a daily routine.

"But Joe, it was raining last night," Adam said, just like a weatherman. I had to laugh.

"And it is going to be sunny the rest of the day," I finished the joke. Adam could take any bad moment, and turn it into a joke.

"Hey man, seriously. You know you can come crash at my house anytime. Plus, I can't understand why you take that crap. If my mom hit me, I would hit her right back. And if she kicked me out, I wouldn't come back."

I stopped walking and turned to look at Adam. "It is not that easy, Adam. I couldn't hit my mom. I couldn't run away, either. She needs me. I'm all she has."

"Joe, I don't get you sometimes. You are like no one else. No matter what, you do what you think is best for everybody else. Why treat your mom so nice if she is such a devil to you?"

I just stood there staring at him, with his black T-shirt over a blue long sleeve one. It was understandable why we were such good friends. We both dressed the same; in dark, freak-like clothes. Our main style was a T-shirt over a long sleeve shirt, with tremendously baggy jeans and tall black boots. Our lips were pierced. We pierced each other's on a dare from another friend. Another dare by Adam's girlfriend left him with a pierced nose. I was lucky enough to have the honor of doing it with a safety pin, but on a payback he did my eyebrow.

The only thing that set us apart was our hair. His was dyed dark purple, and I don't even remember its natural color. He had his hair dyed every color in the rainbow. Mine, on the other hand, was still its natural black. Adam dared me many times to dye it, but I refused. Suzy liked it too much, it reminded her of the night sky.

The bell rang and I started for class, without answering Adam's question about my relationship with my mom. After all, another tardy and I would be suspended. My mom would definitely not like that. Before I could take two steps though, Adam grabbed my arm.

"Adam, I have to go. I don't want to be late. I can't have any more tardies, remember. I'll answer your question later, if that is what you want," I said while trying to loosen his grip.

"I have to talk to you about something," he said, very seriously. Adam never said anything seriously. I felt my heart beat a little faster.

"What is it?" I asked as he let go of my arm. If Adam said something seriously, I knew it was important.

"Your girlfriend, Suzy. She says that you don't like her. She wants to know why you hardly ever go on dates, or even call her on the phone. Why haven't you told her about your mom? Doesn't she need to know?"

"Man, it just isn't that easy. You know that I don't like to talk to anybody about it." I always felt like a wimp when I even only told my best friend about my mom. The part of the city that I come from is rough, and my conditions at home were nothing compared to living on the streets. I thought people would mock me if I told them.

"Well, you have to tell her something. I know you like her a lot, and if she doesn't get some sort of explanation, she might just dump you. You know how chicks are about commitments," and he just left.

He left, and I stood there like an idiot. What was I going to tell Susan Catlett? What if I gave her a bouquet of roses and some chocolate, I thought. Girls love that, don't they? No, I have no money. My last buck was spent on a pack of cigarettes. I can't buy her anything, I have to tell her something. I didn't want to lose her. She is so awesome, and gorgeous.

"Mr. Saleton, what do you think you're doing? Go to class, now!" Mr. Fisher, the driver's ed. teacher was the only one left in the hall, other than me.

"Sorry, I'm going," I quietly responded. I walked slowly to my math class. Suzy was in that class. What was I to say when I sat beside her? Hopefully, nothing. Hopefully, Ms. Sameson would make me go to the office, and they would send me home. I didn't care if my mom went insane, as long as I didn't have to face Suzy. I was there, all I had to do was open the door. Courage should be one of my strengths. I am a city boy.

"Welcome, Pete. I am so glad you could make it. Please, come in, sit, enjoy yourself," Ms. Sameson said, not shouted.

That meant I didn't have to go to the office.

I was about to go sit by Suzy but her friend was in my seat, and they were staring at me. They were probably talking about me. Maybe even discussing my fate.

"Please take out your homework, Pete, and answer number fifteen."

Oh God, no homework, either. Well, I guess I just have to go to the office, I half thought and half hoped.

"Pete Saleton, where is your homework?" Ms. Sameson was getting agitated.

"I don't have it, ma'am," I whispered. When Ms. Sameson was mad, you were in the wrong place at the wrong time.

"You interrupt my class ten minutes after it started and don't have your homework, either! Go out in the hall and wait until I come out to talk to you," she shouted.

I went out and sat by the door. At least I didn't have to face Suzy, but it would have been better if Ms. Sameson sent me to the office. Maybe I could think of a good excuse out here. How about, I've been busy studying. No, no, she wouldn't fall for that, especially after that scene. I didn't know what I was going to tell her. What if...

"Pete, Pete, wake up, Pete," Ms. Sameson was saying. I hadn't even noticed that she opened the door.

"Oh, sorry," I apologized while rising to my feet.

"What has happened to you, Pete? You used to be such a good student. You know that I have to report that tardy and you will be suspended for five days."

I looked at the thirty-year-old lady. Her hair was turning gray in the front, while the rest of it was dark brown, matching her eyes. Her face almost looked like she was worried.

"I know, and I'm sorry," was the only response I could think of. Nobody had ever been worried about me, especially about me being kicked out of school. All the teachers always seemed, almost, afraid of me. Of course I never caused any trouble, but a couple people that I hung out with have made a few threats, only as jokes. Your friends really influence what others think of you.

"And why did you not have your homework? You always do

your work. Is something wrong? Are you having trouble with school, or is it something personal? Whatever it is, Pete, you can tell me. I am always here to talk. Is there something you would like to say?"

For some reason, Ms. Sameson has never been intimidated by anyone before. She never judges anybody. If somebody does something horrible, like threatening her, she talks to them and asks what is the matter, because she always thought that if somebody did something bad, it was because of something personal. She never blamed anyone for anything. Everybody liked her, she was our second mother.

"No," I responded, after some hesitation. I could not tell Ms. Sameson about my mom, no matter how nice she was. I knew that if I told her, she might report it to somebody, but they probably wouldn't do anything about it. After all, almost every family in this city is messed up. The reason I didn't tell her is the same reason why I couldn't tell Suzy.

"Well, if there ever is, you know where my room is. For now, come join the class." I went in with Ms. Sameson and sat down. I did not participate, and Ms. Sameson never called on me. I thought out my excuse to tell Suzy, and I would say it while walking to science with her. It was perfect.

"Class dismissed," is all I heard, and I shot out of that room. It was almost the students' golden rule: Do not stay in the classroom any more than three seconds after you are dismissed. If you do, who knows what people might say about you.

I waited out in the hall for Suzy, and what do you know, she walked out with her annoying friend, Celia. I hated that girl. She hung out with a bunch of my punk friends, but was a total prep. All she ever did was lie like a dog. Suzy hated when I was mean to Celia Karnes, but I think the only reason Suzy hung out with Celia was that of pity for the girl without friends.

"Hi, Suzy," I said like a dork. She gave no response. "I am sorry that our conversation was cut a little short last night, but..."

"A little short! A little short! You talked to me for five minutes, and you didn't even say goodbye. You just hung up on me! You didn't answer my question either, and probably don't even remember what it was! Do you?"

"Oh Suzy, I am terribly sorry. I have to admit that I don't. But..."

"My question was, 'What do you want to do Friday?' You probably don't even know what Friday is, do you?" She was really being sassy. It was unbelievable that I was taking this lecture, without having a word in edgewise, but I really liked Suzy. If you like somebody that much, you just don't argue with them, no matter what.

"Yes, yes, I do," I said with confidence. I thought maybe she would believe me, and I would figure out what Friday was later.

"Well, what is it?" I wasn't going to be let off as easily as I thought. She was too smart to fall for that trick. Suzy never did study, but she had straight A's on her report cards every time.

"Our one month anniversary. See, I know!" That was a total lie. I prayed it would be a good guess. Religion is not my thing, but when it comes to a girlfriend being mad at me, I pray.

"Wrong! It is Adam's birthday. How can you not remember your own best friend's birthday? Remember, we all were going to give him a night he'll never forget. And we've been going out for a month and a half. What is wrong with you?" Her green eyes looked like they were turning red. I hated to see Suzy mad, especially at me.

"That is what I have been trying to explain. We are moving, my mom and I. That is why I don't go out very much. And my mom has been very frantic lately, so she hasn't let me talk on the phone at all. I wanted to tell you, but I wasn't positive yet. I'm sorry," I said, with my puppy dog face. She always laughed and forgave me when I gave that face.

"I wish you would have told me. I'm sorry I snapped at you. Where are you moving? You are not going to leave me forever, are you?" Suzy was smiling now. I loved her smile. It was a sunset to me.

"Of course not, I would never leave you. We are just going to the next block. Funny, huh? It is a better apartment, with less rent." That was a really good excuse. I couldn't help it, I was a natural liar. It comes with the territory.

"Oh, that is fantastic," she said, almost jumping up and down. Suzy always was excited over the smallest things, even if they weren't in her life. I hated to lie to her like this, and then have her be happy about it.

"Let's go to class," she said, while starting to walk. She grabbed my hand. "Are you going to be able to go out Friday?"

I looked over to the babe clinging to me. I was so lucky to have her. She had recently dyed her hair sky blue, and it cheered me up. She was quite short, but a great arm rest! All the guys were jealous that I had her. She was one of the most popular girls in school. "I don't know. It depends on if my mom will let me go out or not. We aren't quite finished packing yet."

"Oh, Petey has to ask his mommy. Uhhh, what a baby," Celia said like a little kid. I hated when annoying preps hung out with the freaks just to try to be cool. Our two styles were so different. Freaks listened to hard core music and dressed in dark clothes. We had different colored hair, pierces all over our bodies, and cigarettes in our back pockets. Preps listened to soft rock or light alternative, and they dressed in polo shirts and khakis. To them, just looking at a cigarette was a crime.

"Shut-up," Suzy and I said in unison. Then we laughed. Suzy didn't mind preps as much as I did. A couple of her friends were preppy, and she had a few preppy clothes. I didn't mind that though, she had her awesome side, too.

The walk home. It's a blast. I am so "lucky" that I am in a neighborhood where everywhere you turn there is another pusher on the corner. They all want more business. They always pester me to buy some, but I couldn't. I enjoyed passing them by. I wanted to go to college, earn money, be better than my parents. Of course I'd tried some, but I only did a little herb, you know, pot, marijuana. I was lucky enough not to have been attached to the stuff; even though it's not addictive, getting stuck on it, like dependent, that opens a whole other doorway to drugs. Like getting totally obese because you can't stop eating, maybe worse. It is also pure luck that whatever pot I smoked was not laced (mixed) with something. I think the greatest luck of mine comes at the fact that the pushers didn't beat me up because I wouldn't buy their merchandise. My life evens out; I can have a bad life at home, but a brain on the streets.

"Yo, Pete! Get yo' butt over here," some druggy ordered. I started off, and just ran. When I looked back, they weren't following me. I figured they had some sort of respect for me, not taking anything. My life might have meaning in the end, and they would be lucky if they lived to be twenty.

I ran all the way home, needing the exercise anyway. My thin tennis shoes were like slippers on the sidewalk. (I had not worn my precious black boots, the ones I stole from the mall. I was starting to regret stealing such an expensive thing, but there is no way I could have ever afforded them. Docs have cushions inside, not my four-year-old tennis shoes with a hole at the big toe.) I took some shortcuts through the alleyways, even though my school wasn't that far from my apartment, maybe only six blocks. When I walked in the door, though, there was a surprise awaiting me.

"Mom, what are you doing here?" My mom was lying on the couch, drinking out of a liquor bottle.

"They let me off early," my mother replied. Then her face turned red in anger when she ran out of liquor. She threw down the bottle and glass shattered everywhere. She jumped off the couch and started screaming. "Why don't I ever have enough liquor? I need some, now!"

She came over and started shaking me over and over. Then she let go and sank to the floor. I knelt down beside her and she was saying, "Why doesn't anyone understand? Why doesn't anyone love me?"

"I love you, Mom," I told her. She always was moody when she drank.

"How dare you say that," she shouted. Suddenly she shot to her feet and started screaming again. "You don't love me! You never did! All you care about are those dumb stars! It was cute when you were little, but now it is just messed up! How could I have such a messed up son?"

Then she hit me, hard. Right on my face. How could a girl hit so hard? Try having two tons of adrenaline going through your blood. I couldn't stay any longer, and so I just left. I could not stand there, let her hit me, and not hit her back. I knew if I stayed, I might fight back; that would be my biggest mistake. I could hear her crying and shouting all the way out the building, but I didn't care. I had enough. Then I ran into Ms. Sameson.

"Hello, Pete," greeted Ms. Sameson. "I could not get your mother on the phone, so I dropped by on my way home. I wanted to talk to her about you, I'm worried about you." She must have been worried about something, for Ms. Sameson lived in the nicer part of town. Seeing someone from her part come over to the "wrong side of the tracks" was rare.

"I... I... I'm going to a friend's house, and my mom is not home," I finally sputtered out.

Then, I heard it. A shot, a gun shot. It did not come from the street, but inside my building. Maybe even in my apartment, maybe my mom. I spun around and raced up the four flights of stairs, and could hear Ms. Sameson following me. I reached my door. I heard no screaming or crying. Maybe she was now calm, or maybe she was taking a nap. I knew that there was nothing bad on the other side, just a drunk mother lying on the floor without any more liquor, but I just wanted to make sure.

I could hear Ms. Sameson panting right behind me. I slowly turned the handle, and walked in. Don't look down, don't look, was all that went through my head. Nevertheless, I did not obey.

Chapter 2

"Oh my God, oh my God." I heard a gasp behind me and then, "I'll call 911."

I didn't know what to do. My mom's face was blown off and I did not know what to do. I just sank to the floor and held her hand. I did not cry, I could not cry. There were no tears. What could I do? There had to be something I could have done.

I felt a hand on my shoulder but heard nothing, just murmurs. Somebody was talking to me but I did not know what they were saying. It must have been Ms. Sameson. All I saw were colors. No bloody face, not my mom dead, just colors.

I put my head on her stomach and closed my eyes. She was

not dead. She would stand up any minute and start throwing things at me. "Start hitting me, Mom, just start hitting," I kept saying to myself. Nothing happened.

I heard screeches, loud screeches. Lots of murmurs, people were there, probably doctors and cops. They could not do anything. They should just leave, but they wouldn't. I felt somebody put their hand on my shoulder and kneel beside me. They started murmuring something but I could not understand what. Somebody else put a blanket on me. What was that for? What is a blanket supposed to do, bring my mom back to life? What is the purpose of a blanket at a time like that?

I started crying. Can you imagine a sixteen-year-old boy from a crummy neighborhood, cry? I never cry, never. Why was I crying then? This woman did nothing good for me, but she loved me. Yes, I suppose she loved me. She was my mother, right? Why didn't she ever show it? Just once she could have said something.

I was frozen in place. I still had no idea what was going on, what all those people were doing there. I felt somebody tug at me, but I could not move. I could not, would not leave my mom, ever again. She needed me and I had just walked out. She needed me when I was not there, when I was running away from her. And now, now she is dead. Dead.

They were tugging harder. They must have really wanted me to move, but they were going to have to take me away kicking and screaming. I was not leaving her. I refused to leave her again.

Despite my resistance, they finally grabbed hold of me. Two men dragged me out of the way and sat me down in a corner. They must have thought I did it, typical teenage stuff. A boy up to no good, doing drugs, and then going off on his own mother. I tried to go back over to her, but they held on. Their hold was no good, though. I squirmed loose, but three more policemen came over and held me back.

I could see them, taking my mom on one of those stretchers. I could not just sit there and watch them take her away. I put together all my strength and pushed, but there were too many of them. They had a grip on me.

"Leave her alone," I shouted. "Just leave her be," and then I lost it. I just gave up, sat back, and burst into tears. There I went with that wimpy crying thing again. Then I felt the men loosen their grip, and saw Ms. Sameson come over. She sat beside me, I put my head on her shoulder and I just sat there and cried to no end.

"Pete Saleton, can you come with me, please. I have a few questions that I need to ask you." I looked up and saw a police officer standing in front of me. He probably thought I killed her. He was right. "Pete, do you have a father or any other relative that you would like to see."

"No," was the short and sweet answer. My dad was gone, forever, and my grandparents didn't want anything to do with me, they thought I was a sin.

"If it is okay, I would like it if you could come down to the station with me. From there we can find a place for you to stay." A place to stay? What did he mean?

"Why can't I stay here?" I had stopped crying, but there were still dried tears on my face. They made my face hard, and it felt weird when I talked, like a cage, trapping my muscles into a tight grip.

"I'm sorry, Pete. I cannot let you stay by yourself, or let you out onto the streets," he sounded like a groundhog. His quiet, squeaky voice annoyed me and I knew I was not going to like this man; I hated groundhogs.

"Whatever," I said. "Whatever" was my favorite word. It feels good in the mouth.

"Good," he said, while helping me to my feet. "By the way, my name is Mr. Pandle." He was even round like a groundhog. I had never actually seen a groundhog, but in elementary school, teachers showed me pictures. I had always thought them disgusting little creatures.

There were still a couple of cops taking pictures of the scene when we left. He led me down the stairs and to his car. There, Ms. Sameson gave me a hug goodbye.

"I wish you well, Pete. And I will come to see you, if that is okay?" Ms. Sameson was a kind person, and I still appreciate it.

Those are the kind of people that make this world a little easier.

"Yeah, bye," I responded quietly.

Mr. Pandle put me in the back of the car like I was some kind of criminal. He ducked my head, just like in those movies. It must have been out of habit, for he apologized for it afterward. The police station wasn't far away, only about five blocks. The whole way there neither one of us said a word. I still wasn't all there myself. Half of me knew she was dead, the other half not believing it. I just had to be careful about which half took full command.

The building was made of dark red bricks. It was tall with many windows close together. It didn't look like a police station, almost more like a school. When I went inside with Mr. Pandle, though, I could tell the difference. Police officers were everywhere. I could hear screams of "I didn't do it!" The books were right, everybody does say that.

Mr. Pandle led me into a small little office and sat me in a plastic chair. "You want anything?"

"No," I said. Looking around the office, I could tell that this man didn't have a secretary. There were files piled everywhere. Even the trash wasn't in the trash can.

Mr. Pandle came back shortly with a file. "So, let us start from the beginning. What happened?"

That was quite a broad question. Life was what happened. I told my story, despite my sarcasm. I started from when I ran up the stairs, to when I saw her lying on the ground. He rapidly took notes and when I was done, he left. I didn't know where he went, maybe to check out my story. I hoped they would throw me in jail. I did not kill her, but they wouldn't take me anywhere else but to a boy's home. Jail sounded like more fun than an orphanage.

In about five minutes he came back. "Other officers found broken beer and liquor bottles all over the apartment. Was your mom an alcoholic?"

I hesitated. I left that part of the story out. It was none of his business, anyway. She didn't die because she was a drunk, she died because I wasn't there for her. "Yeah, I guess so."

"Did she ever go to get any help?" Who did this guy think he was, asking personal questions.

"Yeah, she went to a couple meetings. I used to take her, but one day she wouldn't go in. She told me they didn't understand her. I wasn't about to force her to do something she didn't want to do. Why are you being so nosey, anyway? What does that have to do with anything?"

"Hey, kid," he said, noticing my hatred for cops, and him. "Far as I can tell, your mom committed suicide. I'm just trying to figure out why," he answered. I was hating this guy more every minute. How dare he call me "kid."

"Shouldn't you be out fighting drugs or arresting prostitutes?" All he probably did all day was eat doughnuts and interrogate innocent children.

"My department is homicides. Don't you want to know why your mom killed herself?" His voice rose a little, I could tell he was agitated with me.

"I already know," I whispered.

"Oh, then I would like to be let in on it," he said, like I was a child with a secret. This was no big secret. He should know why. It was obvious.

"Because of me. Is that what you want to hear? It was because of me. I wasn't there for her when she needed me and she died. It was all my fault," I snapped back.

"Pete, don't say that. It was not your fault. Your mom was an alcoholic. Alcoholics tend to lose it when they don't receive help. There could be a million reasons, but one of them is not you. You supported your mom when she went to the meetings and you helped when she didn't. You were a loving son, not a horrible one. It was definitely not your fault," he said, almost caring. "I have to go make some calls. Stay here, and thanks for your cooperation."

He left, and I just sat there. Now what was to happen? Obviously after that little lecture, he wasn't going to send me to jail. What was he going to do with me? I didn't want to go to a boy's home, but I didn't have any other family. The question of what was going to happen to me was all I could think of. All I could do then, though, was sit there and wait helplessly.

"Pete," Mr. Pandle was back. I'm surprised I didn't jump up and down from excitement. "Is there anyone you can live with?

Any relative?"

I thought we had already gone through that. Didn't he ask that at my apartment? "No."

"What happened to your father, or grandparents?" This guy really didn't know when to stop.

"My father left my mom before I was born. My grandparents disowned her when they found out she was pregnant," I said, a little nasty. I was really tired of this man's questions.

"Oh, sorry. I should call a social service worker."

He turned to leave but I shouted after him, "Am I going to have to stay at a boy's home? I really don't want to."

He turned around and said, "Maybe." He left, and my mind went on a rampage. Wonderful, an orphanage would be my new home. Maybe I could run away, but I couldn't do that. I would die on the streets. I would be forced to do drugs, be addicted, have one bad batch, and die. No, I had to follow my dream. My dream was all I had and I just had to stick to it.

"Pete, Mrs. Greene is looking for a place for you to stay. Is there anything you want while you wait? She might be a while, the social service office is always slow. You must be hungry by now." Mr. Pandle was back.

"It's cold in here," was my only response. I wasn't hungry, I hardly ever was hungry. Sleepiness was the only thing that bugged me.

Mr. Pandle went and found a blanket for me. "Here you go. I am sorry, but I have to go out on another job. If there is anything else you need or want, just walk out the door and ask anybody out here for help. See you later." He turned and left. I put the blanket over me and leaned back. So, I was to go to an orphanage. I dreamed.

"Pete, wake up," Mr. Pandle was tugging at my arm. It was hard for me to open my eyes. Sleep had taken over.

"Yeah, yeah I'm awake," I replied groggily after rubbing my eyes. "What's going on?"

"Mrs. Greene, the woman down at the social service office, she is here. She has found you a place to stay. I'm going to let her in, okay?" He sounded like I had a choice to the answer of that question.

"Yeah, whatever," I said while sitting up. Orphanage, she is going to make me stay in an orphanage. With troubled teens and cockroaches. I didn't get along with either.

"Hello, you must be Pete Saleton," a woman of about thirty said while walking through the door. "I am Mrs. Greene. Pleased to meet you," she held out her hand for me to shake it, but I was not about to touch such an ugly person. Her grandma glasses made me wonder how anybody could shake her hand.

"Let me get straight to the point," she said after hesitation. I think she was sorry I would not shake hands with her. It really shouldn't have bothered her, it was the nineties, nobody shook hands anymore. "There is an orphanage in the city with enough room for you. You will stay there until we can find you a foster family. To tell you the truth, Pete, it is doubtful if there would be one available for you. There is a very long list." I did not say anything. Nothing surprised me. So, she continued, "Would you like to come with me? I can take you over there right now."

Again, there was no choice for me. I just couldn't say "no," and then run. This was a police station. All I could do was stand and follow her out.

Orphanages were always places that I dreaded. I just didn't like the idea of one lady replacing ten children's mothers. I always had a picture of all those kids, with their minds elsewhere, wandering around the place, screaming at every leaf that rustled. They probably all had drastic lives to be in a place like that. It just scared me. It scared me because I knew, I just knew, one day I would end up there. With all those kids that had a drastic past, like me.

The taxi that I was in pulled up to a short brick building. There was a wire fence around it, trying to keep all who lived inside trapped. The bricks were almost a pale green due to moss. The windows were small and few. That place reminded me of a prison.

When Mrs. Greene knocked on the tall wooden door, a young woman answered. "Hello, Mrs. Greene. This must be Pete. Hi, Pete. My name is Ms. Belgy. Everybody calls me Ms. B," she held out her hand. She seemed nice enough, better than Mrs. Greene. I shook her hand and quickly let go. I did not want to actually like anybody there.

"I can take him from here, Mrs. Greene. Thank you." Mrs. Greene turned and left, following Ms. B's orders. I could hear her walk all the way down the long sidewalk, each foot flopping after the other.

Ms. B led me inside. "I am glad you are here, Pete. Well, maybe not glad, but happy to meet you. I know that this is rough, many things have happened in the past day. You must be exhausted. I just want you settled comfortably, I know it is late. Would you like something to eat?"

I shook my head. How could I be hungry then? After all that? Her bloody body still lay in my mind, like a horrible nightmare. That is all this is, a horrible nightmare, I thought. Tomorrow morning I would wake up early and make her breakfast. I did think too much, and wild things at that. The dreaming side of me always took hold, and would tell me the exact opposite was true.

"Well, follow me then," and Ms. B led me up the stairs. I could hardly follow, my feet were dragging, one after the other. My eyes felt droopy and my body sagged. As soon as Ms. B opened the door, I flopped down on the bed. Sleep.

Chapter 3

It seemed like a story to me, waking in a strange place, and not knowing where I was. Before the rush of realization came over me, I thought I was still home, lying in my sleeping bag on the floor. Even though the bed was much more comfortable, and the room was actually neat, it still did not connect with me as soon as it would most people.

"Pete, I am glad you are awake," the woman from my dream was back, and she was opening the blinds. Madness struck me, for I was not awake until she did that. When I finally sat up, I looked right into that strange woman's eyes. This dream of mine was surely lasting a long time.

"Good morning," she said, with a slight grin. "Are you hungry? It is almost lunchtime."

I shook my head, and slammed my head back down onto the pillow. Rising out of bed was too much of a task. My body felt like it weighted a ton, and I could not lift it. Then I noticed I was still wearing the same clothes from yesterday. Yes, yes it was a dream. Why else would I be wearing the same clothes?

"All the boys are in school now. I thought, if you wanted, I could give you a tour of the place. You know, so if you have to go to the bathroom you wouldn't get lost." I sat up, and then slowly stood. My muscles ached and my eyes were not fully opened.

"Oh, good. Follow me. I'll show you the bathroom first, so you can freshen up." She giggled a little, but I did not understand the joke.

I sort of stumbled at first, not catching my footing. We went down a hall without carpeting, just wood, and I then realized I was barefoot. The bare floor was cold but I followed Ms. B to the bathroom, despite the minor tragedy.

There was a comb on the sink and I combed my hair. My hair was a mess and I loved to keep it straight. I looked at the boy in the mirror. His black curly hair was frizzy. His eyes almost seemed frightened and his face like that of a lost dog. That was not me in the mirror. I knew exactly where I was: in a dream.

When I walked back out, no one was there. Finding my way to my room, I heard voices.

"I thought maybe he would need new clothes," was what a man said. It almost sounded like the man in my nightmare.

"But he is not all there right now. I don't think he realizes what has happened. If you take him back there the day after, it might not be a good outcome." It was Ms. B. She seemed upset about something.

I sat on the staircase, listening to the voices. Each time one talked, the other grew louder, until they were screaming. What were they fighting about, anyway? It is not that big a deal, me going back to my apartment to find some clothes. What were they afraid of? My mom probably needed to see me, anyway.

"Let's ask him," I heard someone say, and then there were

footsteps. They were coming up the stairs. My eyes were still blurry so I could not see them until they were right in front of my face.

"Hey, Pete. How are you feeling?" Mr. Pandle asked. I said nothing. "Would you like to go back to your apartment and get some clothes, or should I do it? If you do go, I will not keep you long."

"You don't have to go if you don't want," I heard Ms. B behind him. What was she so afraid of? The bogey monster?

"I'll go," my voice was really fuzzy. I guess I was still kind of tired.

"Are you sure, Pete? It might be kind of hard for you." Ms. B appeared around the side of Mr. Pandle. I stood and went to find my shoes. I came back out of my room, a little confused on why everyone was so concerned. I was just going to go see my mom.

Walking up the staircase frightened me a little bit. It reminded me of my dream. I had nothing to be afraid of, though. They were the same stairs I took every day to arrive home.

Mr. Pandle unlocked the door. Why did he have a key to my apartment? It didn't matter then; I was to see my mom. I missed her but I couldn't figure out why. She always yelled at me, and threw things. Yet, I did love her.

When I walked in, I saw it, a chalk outline of a body. There was blood colored inside the lines. What was going on? I looked around. The place was a mess, nothing was where it was supposed to be. Glass was all over the floor and the few pieces of furniture that I had were toppled over. I could see the kitchen from the door; there was no wall to stop a person's view. At that moment I wished there was, it looked like a junkie's apartment.

"Is my mom at work?"

Mr. Pandle looked at me confused, like he did not know why I would ask such a question. I never liked that man.

"Let's just grab some of your clothes and we can leave." He walked over to my dresser but I did not follow. I kneeled down beside the outline. Flashbacks of my nightmare occurred. The gun shot, her bloody body on the floor, policemen everywhere.

"Okay, Pete. I took some clothes for you, let's go." I did not look up.

"Where is my mom?"

"What do you mean? She died last night."

"No, no she's not dead. Don't say that! Is she somewhere drinking? Did you help her find another job? Tell me where she is!" I screamed with all my might. He came over and put his hand on my arm, as if to make me stay there and listen to him.

"Pete, let's leave." He tried to usher me out the door but I wouldn't go. I pushed him against the wall.

"Where is my mom?" I couldn't understand what I was doing. I let Mr. Pandle go, looked at the outline one last time and ran out of there. I did not know where I was going. Mostly for a cool off jog. I could hear Mr. Pandle yell after me as I ran out of the building but I paid no attention. I ran all the way to the school, trying to hide from the truth.

I knocked at her classroom door. I did not know the excuse I was to give the teacher to pull Suzy out of class, but I had to see her. Mr. Cord opened the door. Everybody looked at me and a great silence fell over the room. "I need to talk to Suzy."

"Mr. Saleton, are you all right?" Maybe he knew. Maybe he heard of my nightmare. I nodded my head, signaling that I was just fine. For whatever reason, he let Suzy come with me.

She followed me out of the room in confusion.

I threw my arms around her and squeezed with all my might. There was a slight hesitation for her to do the same. Who could blame her? She did not know what had happened.

"Pete? Pete, are you all right? What is wrong? Where have you been?"

I could not answer, I was almost in tears. What if Mr. Pandle was right, I thought. What if she was really dead? No, no she wasn't. She couldn't be. It was time to stop thinking, I did it too much and too hard. And now I was thinking unpleasant things.

"Pete, tell me what is going on! You did not show up this morning, and then you pull me out of class. You..." I let go and looked into her eyes. I kissed her and stood back.

"I love you. You know that don't you?" I had never told Suzy that before, it was too hard. Guys like me can't share their feelings like that.

"Yeah, Pete. I love you, too. But..." Confusion was on her

face.

"Can you come take a walk with me? I'll explain." A walk would make us both feel better.

"But I have to go to class, and..." I interrupted her the third time in a row. She did the same thing to me the other day, anyway.

"Please, I won't keep you long." I gave her my puppy dog face, hoping it would work. It usually did.

"Okay, just don't take me far." Now it was concern in her eyes.

I took her arm and led her down the hall, not knowing where we were headed. She would ask occasionally where I was taking her but I never said anything. Her hand was almost shaking in fear. I grabbed hold of it, trying to make it stay still. It calmed her down a little.

The cafeteria was where we ended our journey. There was really no other place to go in that school. No one was there, all the lunch shifts were over. Nobody could find me there. The little table in the corner where we always sat when we ate lunch on regular school days was perfect. She sat when I motioned, and looked up at me. Her eyes were confused, and red, like she had been crying. I sat beside her and held her hand.

"Now will you tell me?" How was I to begin? Where in my story was I to start? Was I to admit that I lied to her? Would she understand me?

"I am sorry that I interrupted your class, and took you all the way over here. I just wanted to tell you how much I love you. I hope you feel the same." I am still not sure why I did not tell her the events that had happened to me in the past two days. All I knew then was that if I did not tell Suzy how I felt now, she might not be there the next day to tell.

"Is that all? Pete, you took me out of my hardest class of the day, dragged me out here and will not tell me why! Is that really all you have to say? I thought we cleared that up in the hall." Her eyebrows closed together in that human signal of anger and confusion.

"I am sorry. I just haven't seen you in a while." What other excuse did I have? Should I have told her that I ran away from a policeman? Should I have told her my mom committed suicide?

"I just saw you yesterday. What has gotten into you?" Suzy seemed agitated, the mood in which I hated to see her, even more than anger. She was sweet and all, but once this mood swung in, her roof would blow. I could not look into her eyes. My face shot to the floor and my eyes darted everywhere. I hated to see Suzy mad at me.

The bell rang and she stood up. "I have to go to class, Pete. I really do wish that I could see into your head, to know what you are truly thinking. You should know, I can't help you until you tell me what is wrong. Goodbye," and she walked away. She did not want to know what was going on in my head, I didn't even know. It was confusion, confusion and fright. About what, though? What was I so afraid of?

Not knowing what to do now, my legs grabbed control and led me around the halls. It was so empty in the halls, not even a whisper could be heard. It looked like how my insides felt.

"Pete Saleton, is that you?" I heard someone shout after me. When I turned around, I saw Ms. Sameson standing alone in the middle of the hall. "What are you doing here? Where are you supposed to be?" She walked toward me and I backed away. She was probably going to take me back to that place.

I did not want to face Ms. Sameson, so I turned and walked faster. If I ran, it would seem as if I were in trouble and she would call someone after me. But I figured if I used my long legs, I could still outdo her. It was no use, though, for she ran up and grabbed my arm.

"Are you okay, Pete? How did you get here? Come into my room. We can talk there." There was nothing else for me now, so I followed her like a horse who ran out of his paddock and was now going to be locked in a stall instead. When we reached our destination, she sat me down on a desk. Her questioning started.

"Does anybody know where you are? Where did you come from? Are you all right?" She almost sounded like Mr. Pandle, but his questions were much more difficult.

"I'm okay, I was just going for a walk," I mumbled, but I soon lifted my head and started. "You promise I don't have to go back? You promise you won't tell anybody why I ran away?"

Ms. Sameson looked at me like a judge. "I can only promise if I know what I am promising about." That was enough for me, I liked to talk to Ms. Sameson, except about certain things. Besides, I thought she might be able to help me find my mom.

"I needed some clothes, so Mr. Pandle took me to my apartment. I thought I could handle it, but when I asked him where my mom was, he said she was dead. I don't believe it, Ms. Sameson, I don't believe it. I don't want to go back there ever again; can you promise me that? I just want to see my mom, can I?" After that explosion, I bent my head down and water came to my eyes. I could not cry, crying was weak.

Ms. Sameson came over and knelt down beside me. "Pete, it is going to be okay. Let's just go to the station and find Mr. Pandle."

"Ms. Sameson, is it true? Is she really dead?" My voice crackled due to the emotion hidden in it.

"I think you need to see for yourself. Come on." All I wanted to see was my mom alive, even if she was having one of her fits.

The police station was crowded and noisy. The chair I sat in reminded me of my stoop, cold and hard. I leaned back and stared up, half expecting to see the stars. It was just a foam-cracked ceiling, ugly in nature.

"He was out looking for you. They just called him in," Ms. Sameson was saying. I didn't know why she wanted to see Mr. Pandle. As long as I did not have to go back to the orphanage, it didn't matter. "He will be back soon. He wants to talk to you." She sat in a chair next to mine, and I went back into my own little world, scared of the questions. But even more scared of the answers.

What about Suzy, popped into my head. Should I tell her? She never knew of my family life, would she ever understand? Could I put such a big problem on her shoulders? No, no, she can't know. I cannot pull her into my world. This horrible world with its horrible questions and horrible people. It would scare her too much. It scared me, and not many things did.

I felt a hand on my arm, and a voice in my ear. "Pete, he is here. Mr. Pandle would like us to go into his office." I looked over to Ms. Sameson and finally dropped back down to Earth. I never realize where I am when I go into my world.

We both stood and went into Mr. Pandle's little office. When I sat in another plastic chair, I put my head in my hands. Headaches were my biggest weakness, and my worst enemy. I could stand to be cut in a fight, or break my leg jumping out of a moving car, but I hated the pain of a headache.

"I am sorry if I upset you. It was stupid of me to take you back to a place like that," Mr. Pandle was saying. "Pete, I am truly sorry for your loss, but you do have to realize that she is really gone."

"I can't," I said, with my head still faced toward the ground. "She is all I have."

I heard Ms. Sameson and Mr. Pandle talk about my mom. Her name came up in the same sentence as the coroner's. Then, like they finally realized I was still in the same room, Ms. Sameson talked to me directly.

"Would you like to go see your mom, Pete?" Ms. Sameson put her hand on my back and patted me like a baby. I was definitely no baby.

I sat straight and looked at her. Was she serious? Would she really let me see my mom?

"Yes, yes I want to see her."

The building was built of dull gray stones. It was humongous, and just looking at it, I could sense death. The thought of my mom being in there was too great, but I climbed out of the car anyway and followed Mr. Pandle like a lost puppy. Ms. Sameson had hold of my hand, like a master holding onto the leash.

I was so scared, but much too afraid to admit that to anyone. I was so confused, I had no idea what was happening. There were so many questions, with so few answers.

Taking the ride on the elevator was the worst. It was packed with men in gray clothes. I was glad when Ms. Sameson squeezed my hand. It gave me a small sense of security, like nothing really bad could happen. I was ignorant then.

I obediently followed Mr. Pandle into the square room. File cabinets lined three walls and tables were in the middle. Some woman with black hair opened a drawer. A body lay on a hidden table inside.

"This is Karen Saleton. Cause of death, suicide by gunshot to the brain. Right now, no plan for burial." She had a monotone voice and no change of expression on her face.

Ms. Sameson held my hand tight, but it did not work this time. I put my hand out and touched the stranger's arm. She lay perfectly still and was freezing cold. She had no face, it was gone, and in its place, dried blood. She looked familiar but I could not pinpoint who it was.

"Maybe we should go," Mr. Pandle's voice was faint and far off.

"No, he has to realize it is true." Ms. Sameson always stood up for me, but why then? Why couldn't she listen to Mr. Pandle for once, and make me go? I did not need to know the truth. The truth was too scary.

I realized then who it was, it was my mom. That day came flooding back to me as suddenly as an earthquake. I took my hand away and backed up, turning to run. Mr. Pandle held my arm. I fell to the ground. It was true, what he said was true.

"Oh God, Pete," Ms. Sameson came running to my side. "Are you okay? Come on, let's go." But I couldn't move. Fright had frozen me.

"We just needed you to see. Do you understand now? Do you understand she is dead?" Mr. Pandle really didn't know when to stop.

I did not want to answer his questions. These were too hard to admit. "I'm tired," was all I could say. What else was someone in my position to say?

Chapter 4

Ms. Sameson, is that you?" I heard someone walk across the room and kneel down beside my bed. I felt like I had been sleeping for ages. My throat was dry and sticky.

"Yeah, yeah, it's me. How are you?" Ms. Sameson was

whispering, almost as if she did not want to have anybody but me hear her.

I sat up and rubbed my eyes. It was bright in that little room. Hunger stirred in my stomach. "Food," it said, almost as a command.

"Hungry," was my slow response to the question. Then the events of the past two days shot me like a bullet, and I grew silent. "What time is it?" I asked, just to break the silence. The only thing that ever bothered my ears was dead silence. It bugged me much more than the city traffic, or banging loud music that made you go deaf.

"About twelve. You were really tired, I suppose. You can dress in some clean clothes, they are in the dresser. Come downstairs when you are finished and you can eat something," Ms. Sameson said, still a little quietly. She stood and left, shutting the door silently behind her.

I walked over to the pale green dresser. It was ugly, but in better shape than my dresser at home. I could picture it, the blue dresser standing in front of the wall. The drawers were a pain to open and close and the bottom one hadn't shut in four years. That drawer was where I kept my jeans, hardly ever folded. My mom never really minded them hanging over the side, she wasn't that neat a person, either. Besides, it was easier to find the pair I wanted when they weren't all piled on top of each other.

The house was full of loud voices. As I walked down the long staircase, I grew closer to the shouts and laughs of teenagers. I could hear a few screams of children, too. I hated little kids.

A knock at the front door startled me. I zipped around and just stared at the tall, wooden door. Ms. Sameson came up behind me and touched me lightly on the shoulder, as if to tell me to calm down, it was just a knock. But her attempt of calming me only made me more scared, for I did not know she was there. She walked over to answer the door, ignoring my fright over such a little thing. Suzy stood on the other side, standing as still as a pole.

I must have gaped at her for five minutes before making an attempt to take a step toward her. How did she know where I was? Why was she here? She shouldn't be here. This was no place for her, but when I looked into her face I could tell she thought other words. Her eyes showed great sympathy.

"Come in," I heard Ms. Sameson tell my girl. "Pete, I called Suzy. I thought she should be here with you. I know how close the two of you are."

It was so silent. No one stirred. I could feel that even the air was tense. She did not have any clue of what to say. She knew the story and figured out why I came to school yesterday. And all she felt was pity, not love. She did not love me, I thought.

Yet she walked to me, and stopped five feet in front of me. Was I contagious? If she breathed the same air as I did, would her life fall apart, too? Was she scared to touch me? Scared that her mom would shoot herself?

"I'll be in the kitchen." I could hear Ms. Sameson's high heels patter down the hall. Then there was silence.

"Hey," was all she said. Just "hey," like she would say if we passed each other in the hall. I couldn't blame her. What was she supposed to say? Sorry your mom was a drunk suicide? Sorry you have to live in a place like this? Sorry you're a mess inside?

"You should not be here," I told her straight out. I did not need to have some formal greeting for her.

"I want to be. Pete, I am sorry about yesterday. You were scaring me. Why didn't you tell me? I wish you had told me, not my math teacher. How did Mr. Cord know, and not me? Not your girlfriend, the one you told you loved."

"What was I supposed to say? My mom shot herself and I saw her bleeding all over the floor!" I was shouting and rage just poured out of me. All my anger inside, I let go and dumped onto her. Suzy looked as if she were afraid of me and started backing away. "It is not like everyday gossip, Suzy. It is more complicated than that!"

"I'm sorry," she whispered. She had never seen me mad, and I wish she never had. "I love you, and I just want to help you through this."

"What? Hold my hand while I go through a crowded city and then let go when I reach the country? No, it doesn't work that way. It may never end, and I can't take anybody leaving me in the middle of the street. You only love me now because of pity. It is just pity you feel."

"No, Pete! You know that is not true. I have always been with you, by your side, even when I didn't understand anything. You know that is not true," she sweetly whispered once again. She looked as if she were going to cry. I hated to see chicks cry, but now it didn't bother me. Now, I just didn't care.

"You shouldn't be here," I grumbled. She tilted her head, like all people do when they see a pathetic person. Nevertheless, she turned and walked out. All I heard was complete silence. The shouts had stopped, probably some while ago. They must have heard us screaming.

The hunger had left me once again and I returned to my room. The third door on the left, my new bedroom. I would soon know it mighty well. Maybe even better than my last one.

Just another window, just another wall. This was one time I actually wished I lived in the country. A view of a green mountain, or blue lake, or even a garden would have been so much better than an alleyway. I always dreamed of the country because I thought of it as so much more peaceful. No traffic sounds, gunshots, or homeless people. It is a place to let go of things, to relax, and to look at the stars. It is a place to escape from one's problems, like a family tragedy. Death, even, like my mom.

A knock at the door interrupted my thoughts. A thousand bucks said it was Ms. Sameson. "Pete, are you in there? May I come in?" I guess I owed myself a thousand dollars. I did not answer the questions, but the door opened anyway.

Ms. Sameson walked over to the window and stood beside me. The look on her face showed she was trying to find what was so interesting for me to stare at. I was trying to find it, too.

"I'm guessing your conversation with Suzy didn't go so well," she looked over to me but I kept staring out the window. "I am sorry I invited her over, Pete. I thought you would need a friend, or even a girlfriend. You've been through a lot, and you probably do not think of me as a 'friend', more of a teacher." We both just stood there, looking at the red brick building next door. There was really nothing more to say on either one of our parts.

"Maybe it's none of my business." She looked at me once

more to see if I would reply to that, but I didn't. "You must be hungry. Would you like to come downstairs to eat?" Hunger, eh? Right now that was the least of my worries. "Well, I'll come back to visit you. That is, if you want me to?"

I still wish I had said something. Ms. Sameson cared about me when I needed it most and I just let her leave without letting her know that. She needed to know how much I appreciated her kindness, but then I didn't feel like talking to anybody.

Ms. Sameson walked to the door and, as if she forgot something, quickly turned around. "Pete, I just want you to know I am completely sorry for your loss," and she left.

My pushing finally succeeded. I could never keep anybody close to me, I just shoved them away. Maybe I didn't want anybody near me, knowing how I felt and what I thought. I put myself in the hole and now I could not get out.

It must have been an hour that passed. A nuclear bomb could have dropped and I wouldn't have even noticed. However, the most subtle thing, like a knock, made me come back down to Earth. No one said anything on the other side. Waiting for a couple minutes, I went to go see what was up.

There was nobody standing there, waiting for me to open the door. I looked up and down the hall, and no one stirred. My foot bumped into something on the floor. It was a platter with lunch on it. I picked it up and went back into my room.

"Pete, Pete," someone was shaking my arm. I had fallen asleep again. It was beyond me why I slept so much. Usually I did not sleep more than six hours a day.

I opened my eyes and saw Ms. B. "I'm sorry to wake you, but it is seven o'clock. I was wondering whether you could, or even wanted, to come downstairs and eat dinner with us. I would like you to meet the other children who stay here." Her face looked like she was begging. I could not say no.

I sat up. "Okay," my voice cracked.

When I walked in, everybody grew silent. The room was not what I had expected at all. It looked like a school cafeteria, with the long white tables and plastic chairs. There was even a lunch line.

Ms. B raised her hand, asking for attention, just like a teacher. Everyone looked our way. "Everybody, this is Pete Saleton. He arrived here the other day. Please, introduce yourself and treat him nicely. Show him around. Thank you," and everybody went back to their dinner. I felt like a new kid at school, without knowing anybody or knowing my way around.

They even had school food. Slop, I call it. There were even plastic red trays, and plastic utensils. To top it all off, little cartons of milk. When I took my slop, I looked over the cafeteria. Little kids outnumbered the teenagers, seven tables to one.

Ms. B saw my puzzlement of where to sit, and came over to me. "There is a seat over there beside Rick. He is the one in the blue jean jacket. He's about your age." I walked over to the table Ms. B pointed to and sat beside "Rick."

"Hey, my name is Rick. You can call me Stone, if I like you, that is. This girl beside me is Heather. She's my girl, so lay off." He had a serious tone in his voice and by his dark black eyes I could tell that I should watch not to rub this guy the wrong way. He looked rough.

"Stone," Heather giggled. "He doesn't mean to be that rude. He just gets jealous every time a guy looks at me. Some old geezer passed me on the street and winked at me. Stone here beat the guts out of him." Heather had a light look to her face. Her red straight hair made a frame around her round face. I could tell why Stone was so jealous; she was gorgeous.

It wasn't that hard to start a conversation with those people, they all had something to say. I learned a lot about them, and that place.

The first thing I was told, was how this building functioned. Most liked it here and didn't mind the volunteers that much. They said that the girls' orphanage was right next door, and for dinner they came over here to eat. We had a bigger cafeteria than they did and it was a "privilege" for them to come over. If someone messed up, like getting one of the girls in trouble, then the privilege would be taken away. They warned me to watch what I did, for most of the guys here had girlfriends over there, and they wanted to see them as much as possible.

The strict rules were revealed to me. They were not let out on school nights, but most of them snuck out anyway. There was no strict security here, so it was easy to get in and out. Besides, the only punishment for being caught was no dinner the next night. I could tell many of them didn't eat that much as it was. I also found out they attended the same high school as I did, which didn't surprise me. Some of the people looked familiar to me, but they hung out with each other, so I never really talked to any of them before.

Some of them told me their stories about how they came to live at an orphanage. One boy, Scott, said his dad used to beat him, and he finally ran away. Ms. Belgy told him about this place, and after a while he decided to come. He said Ms. Belgy roamed the streets a lot, looking for homeless kids. She doesn't want a child living on the streets. She gives them information about the place and leaves it to them to decide whether they want to come or not. Her advertisement worked well, for a lot of the kids here found out about the place by Ms. B.

Heather smiled at me, and told me her story. "It was a kind of stupid thing, but do not laugh." I told her I could never laugh at how a teenager came to an orphanage. She blushed, and went on with her story. "I became pregnant, and didn't want the child. I ran away, almost suspecting that the child in my stomach would stay behind, but he followed. Well, part of the way. I had a miscarriage, from tension the doctors said. When I called my parents to ask if I could come back, they said no. So, I came here."

I looked at her blankly. That was definitely not a story to laugh at, and she almost read my mind. She smiled at me once more, almost like an, "I'm sorry I said something that stupid," and then turned away. She was embarrassed by her story and I felt sorry for her that she was.

After dinner, Eric Gaines, a tall goofy-looking guy, walked with me upstairs. "This place isn't all that bad. It is much better than where most of us came from." I said nothing, not knowing how to react. I had a picture of the kids who lived in a place like this; this didn't fit that description at all. They were too nice. "You haven't told any of us where you came from. So, how did you get here?"

I was silent until we reached my room. I did not want to talk about it, especially to a stranger. "It's a long story," I finally said. He looked at me seriously, and then turned to leave. He probably understood where I was coming from and did not want to push me into telling my history.

He turned around and grinned slyly. "It is cool that you can't talk about it yet; most don't want to at first. You will learn to like it here. It really isn't that bad." I nodded, and went into my room. Maybe he was right, but right then I didn't think so.

I lay down on my bed and stared at the ceiling. A sudden urge for a cigarette came over me and I realized I didn't have any that day; I finished my last pack the day before. Lately I had been sleeping too much to even want a cigarette, but right then I felt the hunger for one stir in my stomach. Eric probably had a pack; I thought, I'll go ask him.

He answered my knock immediately and gave me that same sly grin. "Hey," I greeted him. "Do you have a smoke on you?"

He gave a full out smile. "Sure," was his response. "You want a whole pack? I'll give it to you as a welcoming present." I nodded and he went and grabbed one out of his dresser drawer.

"Thanks," I said as he handed them over, "It's cool of you." He shrugged, and I walked away.

"Don't let Ms. B find them," he shouted after me. "She doesn't like us smoking. She might send you to counseling or something." I waved my hand in response, telling him I understood.

The night air was quite chilly, yet comforting. I couldn't see the stars as well here because there was a streetlight, right in front of the building. The sidewalk was hard and cold, but I didn't mind. I was just happy to have a cigarette in one hand and the stars in the other. Maybe that was all I had, but it was good enough for me.

I didn't go back in until I saw the lights in the building starting to go out, one after the other. I stumbled up the stairs, not really wanting to go to bed. Ms. B was heading toward my room when I reached the top of the stairs. She heard me walking and turned around to face me.

"Time to go to bed, Pete. Wake up time tomorrow is eight o'clock, since it will be Sunday. Goodnight," she said while walking to the next door for the same speech. She stopped and turned back around. "Pete, you need to be careful. All the kids here are not as nice as they seem," she paused. "I am very suspicious of Eric. He might be into drugs. I would not like the same thing to happen to you. Please, just be careful." I nodded, not having anything to say. She smiled, and then went into the next room.

I walked into my room and flopped down on my bed. A druggy, eh? That would have been hard to guess with his friendliness. He was probably just trying to soften me up. It wasn't going to work. I wasn't into drugs, I had a dream for myself. Maybe a hope. I could not let Eric know this, though. I still had a reputation.

Breakfast was the same as dinner. Everybody told me more stories and I just basically smiled and nodded. They were still checking me out, to make sure I was okay. I did not want to humiliate myself by saying something stupid.

After breakfast, a kid named Andrew came up to me and stated a proposal. "Eric has some herb stashed. Want to go smoke?" I think it was more, if I said no, I wasn't going to be accepted. If I said yes, they would know I was cool. It didn't seem like peer pressure or anything, but I still wish that I had said no. Just that two-letter word would have saved me from a lot of trouble.

It was cool, though. It had been a week or so since my last social smoke. I could still remember being with Adam and a bunch of my other friends. I wished that I were back there again, with people that I knew, my friends. These new "friends" weren't that bad but I still missed hanging with my buddies.

The place where they hid was wicked. Eric, Andrew, Stone, and a couple of other people led me down the street to this alleyway. I had never smoked in an alley; it was too weird for me. Druggies hung out in alleys, druggies like Eric. It wasn't that scary for me then, though, for I didn't have much feeling about anything I was doing. That was what I wanted, absolutely no feeling. Numbness didn't make you want to break down and weep like a wimp, it gave you strength. It gave you the nerve to do whatever you wanted to do.

After we wrecked ourselves well, we went wandering around town. People knew what we had been doing, and some did turn to catch a quick glance from the stoners, but nobody really cared. It was common around there to be high and go out in public. Everybody did it and nobody cared. Even the cops didn't say anything; there was nothing for them to say. As long as they didn't catch us with the weed, or see us driving, they couldn't do anything.

Andrew went into a gas station and stole some chips for us when we had the munchies. He was quick, and nobody even noticed. I could never do something like that; I would probably fall into something and be caught. I am a really clumsy person and it is surprising that I could even walk down the road without running into a parked car.

When we finally wore off our high, we walked back to the "house." The guys called it that, to give it some meaning. They felt more privileged when they told people they lived in a house. Houses in this city were expensive and it made people think they were rich. I thought that was pretty funny.

It was about four o'clock when we finally walked in. We all went up to Eric's room to listen to music. Well, except Stone, who went to go see his girl. Andrew told Stone that he was totally whipped. We all laughed, except Stone who slapped Andrew hard on the back of the head. I don't think Andrew will ever say anything like that again.

The guys were a lot of fun to hang around. They all liked to goof off. I kind of felt uncomfortable, because I am more of the serious type. It was fun laughing at them though, while they made fools of themselves.

None of us ate dinner, but just hung out with the girls in the cafeteria. I found out that most of them didn't like when the guys went to smoke, especially without them. They didn't want their boys to be in any trouble. Some of the girls were major stoners themselves and could care less. Heather was one of these. Her only response after finding out was, "Why didn't you come get me?" It wasn't that big a deal, for even the worry girls went out and got high that day. They went to the park, much better than the alley. "You are more likely to be caught in the park," Andrew pointed out to me.

I went to bed that night with a satisfaction in my stomach. The people, the place and the events were not as bad as I had thought they would be. I had no other feeling and I had no regrets. Now I do.

Chapter 5

"Pete, a person named Adam is here. He says he is a friend from school. Want me to send him up?" Ms. B had just walked in. She usually knocked, unless she was mad. She was probably mad at me from the previous night. She caught me sneaking in last night, stoned and drunk. All she said was she thought I was a good kid. It took her by surprise.

"Yeah." I was too dizzy to actually walk down the stairs. I had a little too much beer. I never could handle a lot of alcohol.

"Hey, Pete," Adam said, walking into my room. "What's up, man?"

"Hangover," I said without looking up. I was afraid if I opened my eyes I would be blinded.

"Dude, I guess I should whisper." Adam was his usual self, joking around. I couldn't help but laugh, even though that made me want to puke. "I didn't see you at school. Are you not coming back?"

"I was suspended. I was late for class the last day I was there." That wasn't the only reason I was not allowed back to school for the next week. Ms. B told me that the principal said I was acting up too much and he had been thinking of suspending me for a while. He thought it would be smart if I took a rest from school, especially after what happened with my mom. I wasn't about to tell Adam, though, because he would just make a joke of it. He was a class clown too, but he hardly ever was in trouble.

I think the teachers liked his jokes too much to kick him out. He gave a little spice to the boring lesson plans.

I heard Adam come over and sit in the chair beside my bed. Adam hardly ever sat, he was too fidgety. I could tell something was wrong without even looking into his troubled face. I became worried. "What's wrong, Adam?"

"Well, I came by to say I'm sorry about your mom and all. How are you holding up?" That was really weird, Adam hated my mom.

"I'm fine," the biggest lie I've told my best friend. I wasn't great, I was awful. Just plain awful. "But I know that is not the only reason you came over here."

"Yeah, there is one more thing I came over to say." He paused, and all I could hear was my heart beating, pounding in my ears.

"What is it?" He was starting to scare me. I opened my eyes and stared at him, straight into his eyes. He couldn't return the stare.

"It's about Suzy," he said, just like that day in the hall. How long ago was it? It felt like a year ago. "She is really upset."

I hadn't thought of Suzy much lately. I'd been wrapped up in my own affairs, but I still remembered that night. I wanted to call her, I knew I had upset her. But I didn't know what I was to say.

"She was crying the other day in school. She's worried about you, Pete. She told me she came to see you, and you two fought. She said you weren't acting yourself. She's worried about you, and so am I. I think you lied when you said you were fine." Adam looked into my eyes, our first eye contact in a while. I looked into his dark blue eyes. They did show worry, but I couldn't listen. Right now I didn't want anybody to care. If I didn't care, why should anybody else?

"Could you at least go over to see her? Or maybe just call her and tell her you're okay. Please don't shut her out, Pete. She is scared for you, I can tell. You know Suzy does not scare over many things, or cry for that matter. Please, just call her and reassure her."

"Whatever," I muttered. I didn't really care what she thought, or anybody. I was just numb to the world. I liked it that way, then nobody could hurt me.

"Thanks, man. I can tell you're not really talkative, so I'll leave. See ya."

"Yeah, bye," I muttered even quieter. Deep inside I didn't want him to leave. I was lonely there.

I thought about what Adam said all afternoon. I couldn't believe someone cared about me like that. I mean, she was really worried, she cried. I had actually hurt her. I made up my mind, I had to go see her.

I snuck out after dinner. Everybody was in their rooms studying, or pretending to. Ms. B was on the phone in her office. She was too intent on her conversation to hear my shoes pound on the wooden floor.

It wasn't really that long a walk to Suzy's house, but it still tired me out. When I finally walked to her door, I was breathing heavy, and sweating. Luckily, she answered, and not her dad. He didn't like me that much. He didn't like his daughter hanging out with a poor slob like me, much less having her be my girlfriend. He'd worked hard to step out of the slums of the city, and he did not want to be reminded of them.

"Pete! Oh my God, hello Pete!" She was laughing, but I couldn't find anything funny. "Come in." She pulled me in the door by my arm. "My parents are out of town on a business trip," she said, almost reading my mind. I didn't want her to be in any trouble with her dad. She led me to her couch and sat me down. "Want something? Are you hungry?"

"Naw." I took a look around her apartment. It was awfully nice, and clean. Much cleaner than mine was. Both her parents had good jobs, and looking at Suzy it was hard to tell she was in the upper middle class. All the clothes she had were bought in a thrift store. She fit in with the freaks, not the somewhat-wealthy preps. That is why I liked her the most. She didn't believe in money, and if she had it her way, she would give all her money to charity.

"Oh, Pete, I am so glad to see you!" She flopped down beside me and squeezed me tightly. "I was worried about you. Are you okay?" She looked up at me. Her eyes were so soft, they even sparkled. I loved her eyes.

"Yeah, I guess." I was so happy to see Suzy. More so than I showed, but she probably knew that. We could read each other's minds.

"Are they treating you good over there? Feeding you and all?" She sounded like a mother, asking me about nutritional stuff. The weird thing was that she didn't sound like my mom at all.

"Yeah, but they feed me school food." She giggled softly. I loved Suzy's giggle, it wasn't high pitched like most girls, but soft and smooth.

Maybe I was hungry. Maybe I was tired from walking. Maybe it was just seeing her eyes again. Whatever it was, I just broke down. Tears rolled down, one after another, and I couldn't stop them. I kept thinking over and over, crying was weak, I shouldn't cry. Suzy would know how horrible I really felt. But no matter how much I tried to stop, it just made it worse.

I doubled over and started whimpering. She patted me on my back and talked to me in a quiet, smooth voice. "Everything will be okay, don't worry. Everything will be okay," she said over and over. I sat up, still crying, and looked into her face. Worry was all over it. I didn't want to do that to her, worry her. But who else was I to talk to?

"Oh, I'm sorry Suzy. I'm so sorry," I apologized for worrying her. Then I gave up and put my head on her lap.

"Why, Pete. Why are you sorry?" I don't know why those four words set me off, why they made me tell her my story. I think it was because I still "knew" it was my fault that my mom died. I even told her how my mom was a drunk, I had no dad, and life at home was miserable. Suzy was silent all the way through, listening so intently to my every word.

"Suzy, why do I miss her?" I whispered through my tears. "Why did I still love her even though she was so mean to me?"

"I don't know. Maybe it was because she was your mom." She petted me, trying to sooth the pain, and I fell asleep.

Ms. B was not mad at me when I walked in the door the next afternoon. I told her that I went to see Suzy, and she was almost happy. Ms. Sameson must have told Ms. B about Suzy, because

Ms. B said I should go over and visit her more often. She said Suzy was a good person to lean on, which I needed right now. I did not know exactly what she meant, but I smiled and nodded.

The next few weeks went fast. I returned to school after my suspension, but I did not really pay attention during any of the classes. Most people looked at me through sympathetic eyes, which started to bug me. But others, mostly insensitive homies, actually had the nerve to ask me what kind of gun my mom shot herself with. I ignored the questions; they didn't seem to bug me as much as someone might think.

Suzy came over more often and we went out on dates a lot. She was much happier with me, and we never fought. Most of the time we would go out to a dinner or a movie, but all she really wanted to do was take walks up and down the streets and talk. Suzy didn't like to be at home, she did not care for her parents that much. Her dad yelled over every little thing, and her mom was a pig. She wouldn't complain to me about it very much, because she knew that her home was heaven compared to what mine was. I still listened, though; I knew it affected her much more than it would me. She was sensitive.

On one of our expeditions down the road, we decided to take a detour through the park. It was pitch black, and we could not see where we were going. The path had trees on either side of it, making it even darker. I led Suzy off the path and we walked through the meadow instead. There we found our perfect spot to sit and talk.

Suzy was never big on stars. She really never realized their beauty before. It was hard to see the stars in the city, but on that little hill in the park, we could see them as clearly as country people do. That was when Suzy saw their majesty and she suddenly understood what they meant to me.

I stretched myself out on the grass, with my arms under my head, and Suzy used my chest as a pillow. When she talked, I could feel her voice vibrate in my chest. It is the weirdest feeling, an echo almost.

"Pete, what was your mom like, before she was a drunk?" That question came out of the blue. I never talked about my mom with Suzy, only that one time at her house. "I'm sorry, I shouldn't have asked that. Forgive me."

"No, it's okay," I reassured her. It was silent for a minute. I could hear the cars on the opposite side of the park. "She was wonderful," I finally answered. "I can still remember her smile, light and lively. She was scared, though. Scared of what was going to happen to her, I think."

I could hear Suzy's light breathing. We both just lay there and stared up at the stars. I hadn't really paid much attention to them lately. I was too busy with Suzy. It was weird for me not to go out and sit on the stoop every night like I used to, but it was different now. Now I had a life, it was Suzy.

"What happened? I mean, why did she start drinking?" That was a pretty tough question. I asked myself that a lot.

"I'm not positive, but I think it was confusion. Her parents kicked her out of the house when they found out she was pregnant. I think living on her own and then living on the streets was tough enough for her. The fact that she had a five-year-old boy hanging onto her did not help much." I was silent. I did not like thinking about her; it only brought back bad memories. The only good memories I had of my mom were when she would carry me to bed after I fell asleep watching the stars. I hardly remembered it that well, though.

Suzy must have realized I didn't like that subject that much, so she laid off for a while. We just rested there, in a peaceful silence. Then I saw a shooting star. "Make a wish," I told Suzy.

She didn't respond and I realized she'd fallen asleep. I didn't wake her. I thought we had plenty of time before her curfew.

I stared at the stars for what seemed like five minutes to me, which is equivalent to an hour. Suzy's questions had set off sparks in my memory and I started thinking like I did before my mom died. This time it was different, lying there staring at the stars. This time I knew that when I decided to go inside, I wouldn't find her passed out on the couch. This time I would think of my dad in a new frame of mind, a murderer. He was the one who made my mom become pregnant, and stress made her drink, and drinking made her kill herself. It was his fault, not hers. Or maybe it was mine. If I wasn't born, if I had been a miscarriage, if I went first, then she would have lived.

I don't know how long I had dozed off for, but when I woke the stars had moved. The Big Dipper had drifted what seemed like a mile to me. Suzy was still asleep on top of me, and it took a lot to wake her.

"Come on, Suzy, wake up," I said while shaking her. "Your dad is going to freak." She stirred a little, but didn't seem to even know I was there. I pushed a little harder. "Come on, we have to go."

She opened her eyes and smiled at me. Then she all of a sudden realized that she had dozed off, and jumped up in alarm. "What time is it?"

"I don't know, but we better get you back in a hurry. I don't want you to be in too much trouble." She nodded, and we started for the walk to her house, which then turned into a jog, which became a run for the mile. One of the old town clocks rang one o'clock and we ran a little faster.

I walked her to her door and then kissed her goodbye. "Good luck," I said as I left. I could see the fear in her eyes; she didn't want to face her dad. He was big and could scream like a bear.

I took my time walking back "home." I didn't really care what Ms. B thought of my double late curfew; she was not my mom. I liked walking down the empty sidewalk, anyway. It always surprised me that such a big city could be so quiet at night. The only people who were out were the drunks and club hoppers.

Ms. B had left the door open for me, which was a big surprise. It was a rule, if you are not in by eleven, then you sleep outside. She was sitting in her office and immediately called me when I walked in. "Pete, can you come here, please?"

I obeyed and walked into her office. I sat in a chair facing her desk. "I am sorry Ms. Belgy, I didn't mean to be late."

She looked up at me and grinned in spite of herself. "The reason why I did not lock the door was that I knew you were out with Suzy. I made that rule for the curfew for the kids I knew who were up to no good. But I still would appreciate it if you were in before midnight. Could you tell me why you are here so early in the morning?"

"Suzy and I were looking at the stars in the park." I didn't tell her how gorgeous they were that night, but just went on, "We both fell asleep, mostly because of me talking. I had to walk her home, too."

"Well, just don't do it again. I don't want everybody coming in at all hours of the night, or morning. I am glad that you have somebody to talk to, but just be careful. The board, with social services, also has rules. Grades, good remarks from teachers, and a good standard at the orphanage all matter to them. Your grades seem to have slipped greatly and I don't think that going out with Suzy every other night is helping much. If you don't show much improvement, I might have to make you stay in your room and study during the week. Okay?"

I smiled sleepily. I wasn't really paying much attention to what she was saying, I was too tired. I then knew what teachers meant when they told me that whatever they said to me went in one ear and out the other. In between, my brain just didn't catch the words. "Okay," I said in response to the insignificant lecture. "Can I go to bed now?"

Ms. B smiled wryly. "Yeah. Goodnight."

"Goodnight." When I stood to leave, I caught myself and turned back around. "Oh, thanks for not locking the door, Ms. B." She smiled, and I went to bed.

Suzy was grounded for a month after her late arrival that night. We still saw each other at school but we could never go out. To Suzy, that was capital punishment. I, on the other hand, didn't mind so much.

Since I was not going out on dates, I started to hang out with Eric more. He would buy cigarettes for me, he had an eighteen-year-old friend. I didn't have much money, just the fifteen dollars a week for an allowance from the "board." If we made any slip-ups, then they would not give us our allowance until our act was straightened up, almost like a parent. Eric had his allowance taken away a long time ago, but he made his money at poker and pool. He was an awesome hustler.

I started smoking herb a lot more with Eric and his gang. At first, it wasn't that big a deal. A few nights a week after dinner we would go out and smoke a little, but then I started doing it more and more. Soon it was a hobby. That wasn't the bad part.

One night Eric, Steve Cordova (who also smoked with us) and I went to our hiding place. I was taking my stash out of my pocket when Eric stopped me. "I have something better than pot. It works miracles."

"Yeah, what," I said, even though I knew what he was talking about. I was just too afraid to say anything. Maybe I should have said something like, "I like herb the best." Anything not to have gone down that path.

"Coke, ya know, the 'happy go lightly'." He gave me a look like I was stupid, not knowing what he was talking about.

"Cool. I'll go for it." What else was I to say? Naw, I'm a loser. Beat me up now? These guys were tough. If I said something like that, it could be the last thing I ever said.

So I got majorly stoned, and drunk. Forget what happened to me the next morning, with Ms. Belgy screaming and me puking. All she really wanted to know was why. Why did I not listen? Why did I hang out with Eric, even after what she told me? All I could say was that I was just a little sick. What else was I to say?

Ms. B was mad at me for a long time, but that didn't stop me. I still went out with Eric and would have either a sniff or a smoke. It was a lot of fun being *with* the gang; then they were a good set of guys, no matter what Ms. B said. They knew how to have fun.

I became a lot better friends with them. Stone was a wisecrack, and he made me laugh at anything. He reminded me a lot of Adam, who I wasn't hanging out with very much anymore. That didn't seem to bug me much, not hanging out with Adam. My new friends were a lot more tough and cool, they knew the score. Adam was still in his dream world, where I was three weeks ago...

Andrew was a good guy to have on your side, for he could help you out of a lot of trouble. He had connections. Stone and him were best friends, nothing could separate them, not even Stone's short fuse. I think what I liked the most about Andrew is his red hair. It is not bright red, but dull, almost maroon. I had thought it was dyed, but when I said this, I almost had a tooth knocked lose. Andrew was very proud about his naturally colored hair. Stone told me that the last person who denied it was his natural color was almost killed. Meeting Andrew for the first time would not make you think he was that sensitive, but he is.

Steve and I became fast buddies; he liked me for some reason. I liked him, too; he was different from the rest of the guys. Steve had a pretty good understanding of the world, and people. He always had a little glimmer in his eyes, a sparkle. I think that little sparkle finds the good in people for him, not the bad. If I ever saw Steve walking down the street when I didn't know him, I would not have guessed he was such good friends with Eric. Steve had a sense about him, like he was a prep. I always thought it weird that he sniffed, or even smoked. I think he never really wanted to. Maybe that was why we were such good friends; we both had the same hate for the "people" in the world, but the love of the earth and sky. I could tell in his eyes that he had the same numbness that I did, or at least wanted to have.

Chapter 6

I was not keeping track, I did not know that a month had passed. Time didn't seem like an object to me anymore, it just flew by like a plane. It did not bother me, and I did not bother it, until now. For the past month, my new friends and I became tighter as a group. They taught me all I needed to know, that I did not know before, to survive on the streets. I was even becoming a pretty good hustler. Eric, Steve, and I worked together really well.

When I opened the door that night, it all blew up in my face. Time seemed to rush over me like a wave and the past month that had flown by, suddenly came back and knocked me on the shoulder. Just seeing her made me realize what I had done to myself, but I still didn't want to admit it.

Steve and I had gone out that night and had a sniff without Eric. He was out trying to collect donations to pay back somebody who found out he hustled them. Steve and I were never that smart as to stay out until we had fully come back to planet Earth. Yeah, we never showed our faces when we knew we were totally stoned, but once we knew where we were, we would come back "home." That was not the smartest idea, especially for that night.

Suzy was sitting on the staircase when I walked in. I still had that unreal sense about everything, like everything I saw was not really happening, but I was just watching it like a movie. Suzy was just an actress, with those big flaming eyes and red streaked face. She was not mad at me, but somebody else in the movie, the other actor. I could tell Steve felt the same way, for he sat against the wall and watched us.

"Where have you been, Pete?" I looked around the screen, waiting for the actor to pop out and answer the question. "Don't you know what today is? Did you forget already?"

I popped out of my watching stage and I realized she was talking to me. "Huh?" My brain was not functioning correctly to say anything else. It still did not connect the movie to my life. As if Suzy knew this, she stood and walked close to me. She stared into my eyes.

"Pete, where have you been? Were you smoking? Don't you remember that you promised me you would stay away from drugs?" This actress was good. I giggled a little, not realizing she was lecturing me. Whoever she was yelling at was stupid enough not to argue back. "What is so funny?"

I stared at her for a minute. I suddenly remembered the night I promised Suzy I wouldn't do any more drugs. We were walking downtown, and passed this man holding out a cup for change. He could not stand up straight, or even walk, and I could tell he was on something. Suzy became scared, and we ran away from him. "Promise me that will never happen to you," she said. "I know you have done herb, but promise me you will never do anything worse." I promised her because I never thought I would sniff. Things change.

"How could you break a promise like that, Pete? Don't you remember that man, who had nothing more than the shirt on his back and the foam cup in his hand? Didn't you want to leave this city and find a better life? What happened to you in the last month?" She looked like she was going to start crying. I could tell she had done that already tonight. I had nothing to say to comfort her, though. It wasn't my job to comfort her, it was the actor's.

I don't know what came over me, but nothing else would come out of my mouth. "Huh?" Steve laughed, and she left. I asked an idiot question and she left. Who wouldn't? I probably scared her, I was not the prettiest sight. Even then, even at that moment when the only person who I cared about and cared back left, I still did not realize what I had done to myself. Even when the most beautiful girl I knew walked out because of my stupidity, I did not want to admit I took the wrong path. Even then, I didn't care.

Suzy leaving me never took hold of me. I still did whatever I wanted, not realizing the reason why she left. I seemed to be more oblivious to the world, only caring about that moment and not my future like I used to. I think I started to realize that I probably wouldn't have a future, but I didn't care. I finally had my wish, to be numb and not have anyone hurt me.

Every weekend, Eric, Steve, and I would go out to a pool hall and hustle a couple of guys. I think I had more fun doing that than I did when we used the money later. Our favorite place to go was Bob's Billiards Hall. Bob Kedge, the owner, was a really cool guy, and he would sneak us a beer every once in a while when he knew there were no undercover cops around. He was really good at recognizing undercover cops, more so than anybody else I knew. Of course we could all tell, but sometimes it was hard.

It was a regular Friday night, around nine o'clock. Eric's main lesson to Steve and I was to never be stoned or drunk when you hustle; you wouldn't be able to keep your focus and might say something that you would regret later. So, we walked into Bob's straight as a ruler, and headed over to a table for practice shots. Well, sort of practice shots. We were just playing around so people would think we were not that good.

Soon enough, two guys walked in looking for a table to shoot at. All the tables were full and Bob gave them a clue that we were not that good and they should play with us. Bob was usually in on our hustling, unless he knew the guys, heard about them from somewhere, or they were cops. Bob always did warn us about hustling. He told us it would get us into trouble someday, but he still gave clues out. He could never be hurt unless he was the one actually hustling.

So, the two men walked over to our table. One was about twenty, and the other maybe eighteen. The older one had almost as black of hair as I did, and he had deep evil eyes. He wore a tight T-shirt to show off his muscle that I could tell he was very proud of. The other looked as innocent as could be, with blonde hair and blue eyes, and as skinny as could be. They didn't scare me.

"Want to play a game?" The older one was looking at Eric. Eric looked him up and down with his evil eyes. He can look really dangerous if he wants, which is usually all the time. "Whatever," Eric responded, after inspecting the guy's talents. Eric could tell a good player from a bad one as well as I could tell female pot from male.

Eric and Steve usually played while I sat and kept score, but Steve's arm was in pretty bad shape from a fight he was in the night before with a kid at school. Steve doesn't really have a short fuse like Eric, actually he is really tolerant. But this kid told Steve that he was probably in an orphanage because his mom was a whore and left him for the president. Steve is really defensive of his mom, and that didn't make him too happy. The boy he was fighting had about four of his friends right behind him, though. So, I played pool with Eric, while Steve took score.

I had learned a lot from watching Steve and Eric play, it wasn't that hard. First, we played a game risking twenty dollars, which Eric borrowed from Bob. We let the other guys win by ten points; they thought we sucked. The next game we risked thirty dollars, again borrowed from Bob. We only lost by two points and it was easier to challenge these dumb guys again. At first we thought they wouldn't play us for the third time, but they were the kind of guys that never would turn down a challenge from teenagers like us.

Our deal was double or nothing, because these hot shots thought we would definitely lose, even though they were really bad themselves. Our third game went smoothly, we beat the losers by ten points, and they left in a huff after paying up. Eric and I won a hundred dollars, fifty of which went to Bob. I think Steve was more happy that we won than Bob was; he really needed a pain reliever.

Eric went and bought some coke for us. We sniffed it behind Bob's place and then went inside and sat at the bar. Bob said there were no cops around and he would rather have his license taken away than us going through the city making major trouble. It didn't bother us, we needed a place to hang. If any of us were arrested, we would be kicked out of the orphanage and sent to Juvy. None of us wanted to go there, not even Eric.

The place was pretty empty when we went back to sit inside. All three of us are really hyper when we are stoned and we were throwing things around. Bob was yelling at us to stop. He didn't want the last of his customers to leave because of us. His shouting didn't help any. The last couple left and he lectured us on how hard it was to run your own business, especially in this city. Making his customers leave on a Friday night was not the smartest thing for us to do, and he warned us if we did that again he wouldn't help us out in any more hustles. We didn't really pay attention, we were too stoned. We just played some music on the jukebox.

Steve saw them walk in first, and I heard him make a little whimper. His face turned white, and I just thought he was having pain in his arm again. "Hey, man. Are you okay?" Steve ignored my question and just stared at the door. I turned around and saw the guys we hustled before, standing there. They didn't look too happy.

"We aren't stupid, punks. We want our money back," the older one said. He reminded me of, well, me.

"We ain't got it, man." Eric wasn't helping us any. He could have at least given them our leftovers, as little as it was. Eric is not that smart when he is stoned. Steve didn't say anything. I think he knew we were in for it.

"We said we wanted our money," the skinny towhead said this time. He pulled a switchblade out of his pocket. Steve and I backed up a little. We had never had a blade pulled on us before. Eric didn't even flinch.

"I told you we don't have it," he said with a really steady voice. I looked around for Bob, but he wasn't anywhere to be seen. He was probably in the back washing dishes.

"Now what are we going to do about that," the older one asked sarcastically. I had that unreal sense again, like it was just a movie, or maybe I just hoped it was.

"Look, buddy. We won that game fair and square. Now, if you don't mind, I think Bob will be closing soon." Eric stood exactly where he was when they walked in the door. He wasn't scared. Why?

"Our business is not finished yet. We are not leaving until we have our money back in our hands, or until you two look worse than him." The older one was pointing at Steve who had a big blue bruise, swollen eye and busted lip. That was all you could see, though. He also had bruises all over his body from the beating he received from the fight.

I looked around the place hectically for Bob. I was scared, for once, I was scared. Eric, though, stood his ground. "If you know what's good for you, you two would leave."

I don't know why Eric threatened them, they were only going to be more irritated. These guys were rough, and even Eric's tough looks could not scare them away. "Or what," the towhead asked. Eric didn't respond, but took a step forward.

"Let's find out." Eric's words were all that were needed to start the fight. The one with the black hair rushed for me and Steve. He was big enough to take both of us. Steve and I ran for it, but he caught me by the shoulder and started throwing punches. I was never a good fighter, but I tried, anyway. When I kicked at him, he had me down in a second flat.

I had no idea what was happening. I struggled to free myself, but he was sitting on my chest squeezing the air out of my lungs and punching me in the face at the same time. He had on a class ring, not making me feel any better. I could taste the blood in my mouth and all I could think was, I hope I pass out before he kills me.

I thought I was going to suffocate; that guy was heavy. For some reason, he stood back up, maybe to try to find Steve, thinking he was done with me. I stood to stop him; Steve was in bad enough shape. All of a sudden, my arm went behind my back and pain shot up to my shoulder. My eyes were even more astonished, since the man who was beating me was right in front of my face.

I tried to free my arm but I just made it worse. My feet slipped when I tried to squirm out of the grip of the mystery man, and I dropped to my knees, leaving my arm behind my head in an awkward position. The pain surprised me so much that the guy who had a hold of me let go and came forth, knowing I was not going anywhere. My arm dropped limply to my side, and my jaw dropped with it. It was the blonde boy that was beating up Eric. My mind went into a whirl of where Eric was.

The blonde guy kicked me in my stomach and I crumbled over into a ball. The bigger "me" kicked me while I was down, while the other one pushed me over onto my back. Even after I passed out, I knew they were still kicking.

I felt a cold rag run over my face, and I tried to open my eyes. Pain rushed through my body, and I groaned. I felt horrible, like I had been through a meat grinder. My eyes wouldn't open, but I heard a voice.

"Is he all right?" It was Steve. I suddenly remembered that he ran away. He probably wasn't ever caught; they were too busy with me.

"I hope so." Bob's voice was right beside me. He was probably the one making my face sting like a bee. "I think he is awake now."

I couldn't open my eyes no matter how hard I tried. I tried to speak, but my voice was not working. When I tried to move, pain soared through my entire body. I had never been beaten up that bad before.

"Easy, man. You're not going anywhere," I heard Bob say in a soothing voice. "Just stay still, the ambulance should be here soon." I tried to ask why, but I couldn't get the words out. I think Bob knew how I felt, for he spoke to me in a quiet voice, about stupid things, like how pretty the stars were that night. I thought he was making fun of my fetish, but I fell back asleep, anyway.

When I awoke next, I saw Steve sitting beside me. I tried to move, but my muscles were too sore. Steve saw that I was awake, and he scooted his chair a little closer. "Hey, man. How are you feeling?"

It took a lot of strength for me just to talk. "Like crap." He laughed a little, and I tried to smile but my face was stiff. "Where am I?"

"At the hospital." Steve paused, and then told the story of the past night. "When that guy came after us, I ran and found Bob. He had a gun in the back, and came back right after you passed out. He took a few shots, and those guys ran like the wind." Steve tried to manage a smile at the thought of Bob taking shots at people. He was too lighthearted.

"How's," I swallowed. "How's Eric?" Steve looked at me seriously. He seemed to be thinking of something else.

"He's dead." Steve grew silent, and he stared out into space. I knew that he really didn't like Eric as much as I thought before, but it was still really hard on him. "That towheaded one cut him at the throat."

I couldn't look at Steve. I just lay there, staring at the ceiling, remembering what happened that night. Eric stood his ground, and ended up dead. I used to hate Eric; he was too much of a druggy to be liked. But then I had some sort of respect for him, some desire to be as brave as he was. No, he wasn't brave. He was numb to the world, thinking nothing bad could happen to him. He wasn't scared of anything, but he wasn't fearless, just oblivious.

I heard someone come in and tell Steve he had to leave. I didn't face them, but just kept on staring. I was too tired to move my head. "See ya, man." I fell asleep soon after.

Only two people came to see me in the hospital, Steve and Bob. Ms. B did come a couple of times, but Steve was there all the time. I think he was still scared something bad would happen to me, like it did Eric. He wouldn't admit it though; he would just sit there and try to make conversation.

I was happy to see Bob come in; he was an awesome guy. He didn't seem too happy to see me like I was, it scared him a bit. At least he wasn't the one in the bed flinching from the pain. Nothing was majorly wrong with me: a broken arm, concussion, slight fever and major bruises on every part of my body. They, the doctors, just wanted to keep me in the hospital for a couple of days to run tests and make sure my head was okay. Well, physically, that is.

"Hey man, how are you?" Bob greeted me as he walked over to my bed. His fists were jammed into his pockets, and he had a lost look on his face like he did not know what to say.

"Better than the other night," I whispered. I couldn't talk too loudly, I didn't have that much energy. My voice was just coming back, too. When he grinned, I tried to smile, but my face was really sore.

"I heard you were going to be fine. I tried to warn you losers about hustling. Why didn't you listen?" He laughed a little. I could tell he was really uncomfortable. He sat in the chair beside my bed, trying not to be so nervous.

"I don't know, man. We were just looking for trouble." It was quiet for a minute. "You still have your precious business?"

Bob looked at me and tried to smile, but I could tell he was upset about something. "I told you guys that I would rather have my license taken away than you all making trouble in the city. It didn't help any, both happened."

"Oh, I'm sorry. Why did the cops take it?"

He laughed. "Possession and letting minors in. Eric hid some of his leftovers behind the counter, and I didn't know about it. If I did, I would have belted him good. He isn't that smart."

"You mean, wasn't." I looked at Bob who stared at the floor. He wasn't too happy about Eric, either.

"Yeah, I guess I do." We were silent for a while. I could hear the shuffling of people's feet in the hall. "I'm sorry about Eric," he finally said. "I should have been there. I was too late."

"It wasn't your fault. He was asking for it. He wasn't scared of them, he just stood his ground and almost begged them to jump on him." Bob looked at me seriously and I continued, "Eric was my friend, but I will testify that the coke they found was his, and mine. The worst thing that could happen is I go to Juvy. It's not like I'm going anywhere else. I couldn't stand seeing you losing your business; it means too much to you. I have nothing to lose, neither does Eric. It couldn't have been that much, anyway. Steve sniffed a lot, he was in pain." I stopped and took a breath. I stared at the ceiling. Talking wore me out, and whatever pain killer the doctors gave me was wearing off.

Bob put his hand on my arm like he was concerned. He could tell I was in much more pain than Steve was. "Don't say anything to the police. I think they knew it wasn't mine; they found it in Eric's blood, and yours. They only took away my license because you three were in the bar, not really because of possession. That is all that is going to happen to me; I will apply for another one in six months. They'll think I learned my lesson. Until then, one of my friends is going to buy my business from me, but he will let me buy it back. If you confess, you could go to jail. Jail is not a nice place, trust me. No, don't say anything."

I was quiet for a minute. "Thanks, man." I turned and looked at Bob. His eyebrows were tight together because he was worried that I would tell the cops.

"For what?"

"For everything." He knew what I was talking about, and stood to leave. Something stopped him, and he turned back around.

"Get better. I'll see you around, okay?" He smiled. "Oh, and try to stay out of trouble." He left, and I happily went to sleep.

Ms. B came to pick me up. I was happy that I was leaving the hospital, it smelled in there and the food was horrible. I was also quite shaky from not having enough coke for a week. Steve did bring me some coke, but only a little, and only once. It was just to hold me over until I could go home. The doctor would not let me leave that easily, though.

"Before you go, Pete, I have a few things to say." The doctor was not too anxious about letting me leave; he was worried I would see him again soon. "First, take it easy. Don't jump back into things too early. Stay in bed for a couple of days, maybe even up to a week might be best. Next, be careful. I don't want to see you here again, you understand? Well, except to take that cast off." He smiled at me, and then turned to Ms. B. "Watch him, okay? Make sure he eats. He did not eat that much while he was here, but I wasn't too worried. He did have a fever. And," he whispered like he did not want me to hear him. "And talk to him about what happened. The psychological effect of this worries me the most."

"Okay. Thanks again," Ms. B said. We left after she signed the release papers.

"I'm glad you're okay, Pete," she said as we caught a taxi. "I was worried about you. You scared me. You scared the whole orphanage." We were quiet the whole way back. Neither of us had anything to say.

After Ms. B paid the driver, I turned to her. "Thanks for not giving me a lecture," I laughed. She smiled, too.

Everyone was waiting in the front hall. I was glad to see them all, even Steve who I was almost sick of. He came to visit me all the time and would always apologize for running away. I kept telling him I was glad that he did, because that guy would have killed me if Steve had not found Bob.

"Welcome home, Pete!" Everybody's shouts made my head pound. My head still hurt a lot, but I smiled anyway.

"Hey everyone." I looked around. Even the girls were over. They all smiled, and I could tell they all knew the story. It was kind of humiliating, being beat up so badly by two people. Steve was not half this bad, and five guys beat him.

"Okay, everyone, it is time for Pete to go to bed." They all laughed, and I could feel my face turn red. I felt like a little kid. They all left, though, and I went to my room. My head was really pounding, and I took a couple pain killers that the hospital gave me. Ms. B came in and saw me swallowing the horse sized pills.

"I'll take those." She smiled while taking the pill bottle out of my hand. "I wouldn't want you to become addicted to these, too." I didn't think that was as funny as she did. "I just came up to ask if you were hungry."

"No." I was angry she took away the pain killers. I was in pain.

"Okay. If you need anything, even these, you know where I live." She laughed at her own joke, but I just stood there with a frown. She got the clue, and stopped smiling. "Have a nice nap," and she left.

I changed and climbed into bed. The pain killers were just starting to take effect, but I was still shaking. I needed something else. Steve must have known, because he walked in the door.

"Hey man. What's up?" I managed a smile, but all that was on my mind was sneaking out and having a sniff. "We're all glad you're back."

"That's cool. Hey, Steve, do have any coke on you?" I always did say things bluntly. I hate beating around the bush, but I love that term.

"I thought that was what was wrong with you. You are pretty shaky. Yeah, I have some you can have. I can help you sneak out, if you want."

"Yeah, I need it badly." I followed Steve out of my room and down the stairs. He was pretty good at sneaking out. He listened for footsteps, but everybody was somewhere else. We ran to Ms. B's door, and he looked in. I could see him relax and I knew she wasn't in there. We ran all the way to our hiding place despite the known fact that no one was after us.

"Here you go, man." He lighted a joint for me and handed me the bag of coke. Just the look of it made me almost jump with glee. I thought I was going to die if I didn't have any coke by that night.

"Thanks. You have no idea how much I need this." He laughed, and lit a cigarette. I looked over to him in a questioning way. "I thought you didn't smoke. You said you couldn't stand the taste."

"I changed my mind." He was silent, and when I tried to offer him a sniff from the coke, he refused. "You probably think I went weird after he died, don't you?"

"Naw, man. It's normal, cigarettes, I mean. It's cool you don't want to get stoned, too. I don't blame you, after that close call." I laughed.

Steve didn't say anything for a while, until I was finished with my bag. I felt a lot better after I sniffed it. I stopped shaking and just lay back in pure bliss. He was pretty quiet, but that didn't bug me. He just lost a friend. I thought I should talk to him about it, though.

"Steve, I am sorry about Eric, but don't let it get to you. He was asking for it, you know that. I wish I could have stopped him from making them mad. He must not have been thinking right."

"No, he was thinking just fine. And even if you or I had tried, we couldn't have stopped him. He did what he wanted to do, and I think he is happy about what happened."

I was quiet for a minute, trying to figure out what Steve was talking about. "What do you mean?"

"He wanted to die, he wasn't happy in the least. He hated the world and didn't want to live in it anymore. Those guys just gave him the chance he was waiting for, to go down in style. I saw the towhead from behind the counter; Eric did not try to fight him back. He knew if he did he would win, and that was one fight he wanted to lose. You were just in the wrong place at the wrong time. I know that you are the last one he would want to be hurt in his glory, he liked you."

I dwelled on Steve's words. That was why the towhead came over to start on me; he was finished with Eric. Then another thing came to me. "What do you mean he liked me?"

"Exactly what I said. He thought you were awesome, we all do. You are fearless, but not oblivious like Eric. Stone was the first to say that he was sorry you were caught up with us. We all think you could go somewhere in life, but not now. Now you're in too far over your head." Neither of us said anything after that. I thought about what Steve said for a long time, but soon forgot. I went into my painless world and fell asleep.

Chapter 7

"Come on Pete, wake up. We have to go back." Steve was shaking me, but I didn't want to open my eyes.

"Leave me alone and let me sleep." I rolled over and felt the cold concrete on my face. Steve kicked me on my back, and I jumped onto my feet. "What do you think you're doing? You hit me on my bruise!"

"I'm sorry man, but we have to go back. I fell asleep, too. We missed dinner, and Ms. B definitely knows we are missing. She is going to scream her head off." I knew I was thinking the same thing as Steve. If Eric was there, that would not have happened.

We ran back. Ms. Belgy was sitting on the staircase when we walked in. She stood and her face went tight and red with anger. We walked in and shut the door hesitantly.

"Where the hell have you two been?" We jumped back a little. I never heard Ms. B say anything bad, not even hell. "I walked into your rooms to find you gone. What do you think went through my mind? I was ready to call the police when you two just strolled in. Tell me where you have been!"

"We're sorry. I wanted to go outside, and Steve came with me. We went down the road, and I fell asleep. He went to sleep, too," I said quietly.

"Pete, why didn't you tell me you were leaving the house?" She almost seemed relieved that we weren't doing anything horrible, but I still don't think that she bought it. "Go get something to eat, Steve. Pete, I want to talk to you in my office."

Steve gave me a little pat on my shoulder as he left, telling me good luck. I was reluctant on following Ms. B into her office, I hated to be lectured.

"Take a seat, Pete. I have a few things to say." We both sat, and she started. "The board is considering on kicking you and Steve out. I told you one of the major rules was no drugs at all. I found marijuana in your bedroom, and when you were at the hospital you had more drugs in your system than they do at the pharmacist. And they sent me a letter from your school. They are going to expel you because of too many cuts and skips. They said you were in too much trouble. What do you have to say for yourself?"

"Not much. I just want to know who the board is."

"I used to like you, Pete, before you cocked this attitude." I flinched a little. I hated people to tell me that; I never liked to be troublesome, but then again, I didn't care about anything anymore. "While you were in the hospital, I reviewed your file. You never told me you had relatives. In fact, you never told Mr. Pandle that, either. Why?"

"I did tell Mr. Pandle. I'll tell you, too. My dad ditched my mom when he found out she was pregnant. I never met my grandparents, they disowned my mom. And why would I want to meet my dad's parents?"

"Oh, I'm sorry." She heard the hate in my voice, she knew what I felt for my "relatives." "Pete, one more thing. The board won't kick you out if you go to rehab. I don't want you to leave, I have faith in you. You have potential, Pete, and drugs are not going to help you at all. Please go."

I looked at her through thin slits in my eyes. How could she ask such a thing? "No," I said bluntly. "I am not addicted to anything. I will not go to rehab, bad people go there. I am not bad. I am just a teenager. It is just a stage, or something."

"Pete, how can you say that? I am not stupid, I know what you have been doing for the past two months with Eric and Steve. I was too afraid to confront you with this before. You are smart, you should know that teenagers can be addicted, too. Not only bad people go there; I am not saying you are bad. I am just saying you need help. I will not have drugs in this place, little kids live here, too. Please just think about it." I stood to leave, but Ms. B called back. "There is one more thing, it is about Steve. His file has been reviewed, and the same thing goes with him. His chances of leaving are much greater; I have been suspecting him for a while. Try to think of going to rehab. It is your only chance. Talk to Steve, too."

I left and slowly walked up the staircase. I had my mind made, I wasn't going to go to rehab. I could live on the streets, I knew how to take care of myself now. Maybe Bob would let me crash at his place, I thought. I went to Steve's room; he had to know about this.

I walked into his room. He was lying on his bed staring at the ceiling. "Hey Steve, what's up?"

He did not move, but I heard his quiet voice. "I'm cool." I was worried about Steve. I wasn't worried about anything, I didn't cared about anybody but myself, but I was worried about Steve. His friend died, and he was acting like I did when I finally admitted to myself that my mom was dead. That was not a good state to be in.

"I just finished listening to Ms. B nag at me. It wasn't half as bad as I thought it would be," I lied. It was worse than I thought it was going to be. I went over and sat in a chair beside Steve's bed. "There was just one thing. She is considering kicking us out. She looked over our records and..."

Steve shot up. "What do you mean? Did she say anything about..." He turned white.

"No, she didn't. Don't worry about that. You already won, they can't bring it back up again."

"Funny, ain't it? I mean, you know, I thought that all that was gone. They always say your past comes back to you, right?"

I knew exactly what Steve was talking about. One time Steve and I went out and smoked a joint without anyone else, and we told each other our stories of our past. His seemed far worse than mine. It didn't seem like he was doing drugs by choice.

When Steve was one, his father was killed. He had been run over by a bus. His mom remarried to some creep when he was six. This guy would beat up his mom in drunken rages, and usually Steve, too. Steve was too young to know exactly what was going on. He couldn't fight back, and was too scared to run away. As Steve grew up, he grew smarter. He hardly fought back, for his mom asked him not to. Steve would never disobey his mom, like me. To get away from his stepfather, he would just crash at a friend's house for a couple of days. The only thing that drove him back home was to see if his mom was okay.

Every time Steve did go back, his mom was worse, and the jerk was drinking more. Steve begged his mom to leave this guy, but she couldn't. She said it was too late; if she left now, he would kill her. The only thing Steve could do to not blow up this guy, was leave again.

Steve knew Eric before they came to the orphanage. Eric introduced Steve to herb. Steve told me he did not want to ever do drugs, but he was scared of Eric. Eric was a real tough kid, and he would never accept no as an answer. So Steve did whatever Eric gave him.

One time Steve was bruised up from one of his adventures at home. He told Eric, and Eric took it coolly enough, having a father that beat him, too. But the next day, Steve was arrested.

A whole trial followed, trying to convict Steve of murdering his stepfather. His mom's testimony proved that he shot himself, so the case was closed. His mom killed herself soon after.

Steve was taken to the orphanage. Eric soon followed, thinking it would be good business. Steve had hoped he would stay away, but Eric was an old time druggy. He had to follow his customers. Steve never could say no, especially to Eric.

"Hey, Steve. Don't worry about it. They found you innocent last time; I'm sure they won't bring it up again." Steve dropped his head and stared at the floor. I could see his hands shaking a little.

"There was one small detail I never told you, Pete. I know who did it. You might be able to guess." He looked up and smiled at me. I knew, but I didn't say. I just nodded my head. "It was kind of my fault; I should never have told him. All dealers give their customers some form of false security. They want you to think they will protect you, not let anyone hurt you. He ended up hurting me more than that jerk of a stepfather could ever have.

"Like I told you before, when I told Eric, he took it lightly. No biggy, right? But when I saw Eric the next day, I knew. I knew he shot him and somehow made it look like it was suicide. My mom must have been out or something, which is why she didn't know. I don't know why she jumped out of that window. Maybe he brainwashed her so she thought she needed him. I'm glad he's dead, and sometimes I think that Eric didn't do it for my business. His father used to beat him, and he always told me he wanted him dead. Maybe he killed my stepfather and pretended it was his own father."

There was silence in the room. Neither one of us said a word. Steve put his head down on his pillow. He was trying to hide the tears. Guys like us don't cry, except I think Steve now knew that we were too good of friends to care if the other cried.

"There is one more thing, Steve. Ms. B wants us to go to rehab. She says that is our only way to stay. But I refuse to go. I think we should run away and maybe stay with Bob." Steve sat up in a flash.

"No. We have to go. We have to try to be rid of this, this, this crime. I don't want to live on the streets, and I know you don't, either. We must go." Steve had tears still flowing down his cheeks, but he made no noise.

"Why? Why should we go? Bad people go there!"

"No! Bad people don't go there," he shouted. "People who are smart do. We have to try to get better. Be smart about this one, come with me. Remember when I told you everyone was sorry you became friends with such losers? Well, now you have to prove that you can go somewhere. Besides, if you don't go willingly, I will drag you out the door."

I smiled at him in spite of myself. I could just imagine little Steve dragging me kicking and screaming. Steve was not scrawny, but definitely smaller than me. He was about two inches shorter and he weighed twenty pounds less than I do.

I thought about what Steve said, and left to return to my room and let him be. He had to soak all of this in. While I lay on my bed and stared out the window, I remembered something. I used to have a dream, to be better than my parents. I was going to go to college, find a job, have money. To me, that was loser stuff now. But I couldn't be like my dad, running away from every challenge.

I made up my mind to go with Steve to rehab. Besides, I knew if I didn't I would either be a punk who ran away from his family, or dead from a cut at the throat. Ms. B said I had potential, I just had to use it. I had to see what I could really do with my life.

I walked down the stairs slowly. My heart beat a little faster because I did not know what to say to Ms. B, or how to say it. I walked into her office and just stood inside the doorway as still as a rock. Ms. B looked up from her desk, she was writing something.

"May I help you, Pete?" I couldn't say anything, my throat tightened a little. "What is it? Come sit and tell me." She motioned toward the chair, but I just stood in the same place.

"I... I just wanted to tell you that..." I couldn't actually say it. Why was I doing this to myself? That question went over and over in my mind; I didn't really want to go.

"Yes, Pete. What is it? Just say it." She looked at me, confused. She was trying to figure out what was going on in my head.

"I will go," I finally spurted out. "I mean, I will go to rehab. And so will Steve." There, I said it. That was final. No turning back now; I'm in it for the long run, I thought.

"Oh, Pete! That's great! I'm so happy you made the right decision!" Ms. Belgy jumped out of her chair and ran over to me. She was almost jumping up and down. She gave me a tight squeeze, but I just stood there, not really knowing what I had done. I didn't really want to go; I think I just agreed because of what Steve said. He was my best buddy.

"Don't worry, Pete. Now I know everything will turn out perfect." She let go of me and looked into my eyes.

"Who's worried?" I asked, and she laughed.

It wasn't that much fun in rehab. The people there wouldn't even let us smoke cigarettes. They said it was "knocking two bad habits down with one stone." That didn't help my nerves any.

We had our own rooms, Steve and I. But sometimes we saw each other, in the halls, during meals, or at exercise time. Steve never looked that good to me, but he always told me that this was for the best. Whether that was to reassure me, or just to reassure him, I will never know. I was more scared when I saw him with his ghostly pale face than I was when I looked at myself in the mirror. His eyes caved in from no sleep and he drooped around. I knew the pills they gave us to help us sleep weren't helping him at all. They were probably making it worse.

I didn't talk to anybody there except Steve. Some of the nurses thought I was deaf because I never responded when they asked questions. They finally figured out I was just hating it there and I would not converse with any of the people. They soon stopped trying to be friendly.

I went to therapy. The shrink was pretty cool; he had hair like Einstein's and glasses like Elton John's. But no matter how much I liked him, I still refused to talk. I had a pact I made to myself not to talk to anybody there. Plus, I don't like talking to strangers about my problems. Mr. Anderson, the shrink, would talk to me even if I did not respond, though. He would mostly talk about his family. It was more therapy for him than me, but I didn't mind. He had an interesting life.

One time when I walked into his office, he had a surprise for me. Usually he sat in this big brown leather chair, but that day he was sitting behind his desk. He had one vanilla file in his hands, and he kept staring at it, even after I sat on the couch, which I loved. He did not talk for five minutes, but finally rose and walked over in front of me.

He stood there holding the file and not saying anything. He handed it to me, and motioned me to open it and look at what was inside. I did, and found some disgusting bloody pictures. I knew who they were of, me. It was my police file. The first picture was when I was beat up by the men at Bob's bar. The other was one of when I was six years old.

My mom was never really horrible to me, but one time it was worse than usual. My mom had just started drinking and her body wasn't used to it yet. We were staying at the shelter, and on Tuesday nights there weren't that many people there. She had too much to drink and was in one of her violent moods. She took me to another room and started throwing me around and hitting me. I screamed, but nobody heard me. She busted the end of a bottle and cut me up pretty bad. When she went to throw me against the wall to knock me out, somebody came in.

I had to stay at the hospital for a while. When the social services came to ask me if I wanted to find another home, I said no. I still loved my mom, for some reason. I was only six and didn't know what was going on. One minute my mom was beating me up, and the next she was holding my hand in the hospital. She didn't mean what she did, and so I never brought it up to anybody, ever. It would only cause more trouble.

"You had it pretty rough, huh?" Mr. Anderson looked down at me while I stared at the pictures. I was amazed to see myself in such bad shape. "Why did you stay with her?"

I put the pictures back in the folder and looked up at him. "What do you mean?"

He knelt down so he could look in my eyes at an even level. "I mean, the report in there says you didn't want to leave her. Why?"

I went quiet. That was a hard question to answer. "I loved her, she was my mom. She needed me. I was all she had."

He stared at me, and I took my eyes away and looked out the window at a passing bird. I wished then that I could fly. I would fly away from there, away from that folder, away from those questions. "It wasn't your fault."

I looked back at him. "What?"

"It wasn't your fault. It wasn't your fault she did that to you, and it was definitely not your fault she killed herself." I stared at him. This guy sure did have a puzzling way of talking. I did not mention once to him that it was all my fault.

"What do you mean?"

"I mean what I say. It wasn't your fault." I tore my eyes away again and stared at the floor. I had told myself that many times, but I had never believed myself.

"I know," I said bluntly. Mr. Anderson stood and looked at the wall, and then back down to me.

"I don't think you do. If you did, you probably wouldn't be doing this to yourself. You're a smart kid, Pete. I can tell that without even hearing you tell me anything about yourself. Your only problem is you are still blaming yourself, even if your brain tells you different, you still blame yourself. Listen with your heart; it wasn't your fault. None of it." He started to speak with a little more power behind his voice. He seemed more scared than I did.

I stood up to face him. "I have to go to the bathroom." I walked away, but he grabbed my arm.

"You're not leaving until I know you understand. It wasn't your fault, Pete. It wasn't." I turned around fast and smacked him against the wall. He stood straight again, even though I hit him with all my might. "Violence won't help you this time. You must listen; it wasn't your fault."

I walked over to him and held him by the collar like I did to Mr. Pandle when I wanted to know where my mom was. "Why don't you leave well enough alone?"

He breathed heavily. I knew he was scared of me, but he still wouldn't stop. "Because I want you to believe me. Believe that it wasn't your fault."

I let go of him and stood back. This guy wouldn't stop. "Then why," I whispered. "Then why did all of this happen. Why is she dead?" I picked up the folder from the couch and threw it against the wall. It just missed his head.

"Because she had problems and, if you're not careful, yours will be worse than hers. Her solution to the world as a whole was, 'have a little drink and make it all go away.' She never thought of the consequences or what would happen to her only child. It was not really anybody's fault, just society's, but it definitely wasn't yours!"

"Why do you keep saying that? I left when she needed me. I ran out the door like my father when she needed somebody to lean on. If I had just stayed, she would still be alive and I wouldn't be here!"

"Wrong, Pete. Maybe she didn't die. Let's just say that. Then she would just get worse and start making your life such a living hell that you would run away from home by doing something worse than drinking, like drugs. Say nobody took you off the streets, and you just did even more than you have already done. You could have wound up dead before she did. Then what?"

I stared at him. I didn't have to take that crap. I ran out of the room, and outside. I didn't want to hear that. It couldn't be true. Yet, I knew deep down inside, it was.

Chapter 8

I didn't have an appointment when I walked into his office. I just needed to talk to him. I thought that maybe he could help me. Mr. Anderson seemed happy to see me, but he never said anything. He just sat there, and looked up at me.

"Hello, Pete. May I help you?" I stayed at the doorway and looked over at him, straight in the eye. It seemed funny to me how shrinks hardly ever changed the expressions on their faces.

"I'm sorry." When he stood, I backed up a little bit. I didn't need him to start yelling at me again. He probably knew how nervous I was, for he talked in that quiet easy voice.

"For what?" He walked closer to me, but when I backed into

the hall, he stood still.

"For hitting you. I didn't mean to, I was just mad." My heart was pounding a little harder. I knew he would start talking about her, and I hated to talk about what happened.

"That's okay. It comes with the territory. Come in and sit. My next appointment is not for another hour. Consider this one a bonus." He smiled a tad, and waved me into the door. I hesitantly went in and sat on the couch. It sank when I sat because it was old and had few coils left inside. That was what made it so comfortable. "Do you want to talk about it?"

I looked at him. He sat in his brown chair. I knew he wouldn't bring the folder out again. I had nothing to fear, it was just my past. Yet, it still hurt a little. I sank down further and put my head on the back of the couch and closed my eyes for a minute. When I opened them, the white ceiling seemed like a movie screen. I could see all that happened to me, but I saw it through Mr. Anderson's eyes.

"I was only six and scared out of my wits," I started. "We had lived on the streets, and I had seen more than most grown adults have. She didn't really want to stay at the shelter, but she knew that was her only choice. It upset her so much, being a teen mother living on the streets. She thought alcohol could put away all her worries. She didn't mean to do what she did, she was just not thinking clearly. I know she must have loved me. I was her son, right?"

"Yeah, Pete. That is right." I didn't look at him when he spoke, but just kept on with what I thought had to be said, and what I had to finally let out.

"She never beat me like that before, and she never did it again. Yeah, she would smack me around, and throw things at me, but it was never like that. I loved her, and I stayed with her in hope that she would try to quit drinking. But she didn't. I don't really know why I stayed even after she seemed to worsen, but I did."

"Pete, it is kind of like a dog that is constantly beat by his owner. He still comes back for hope of his master giving him a pat on the head this time, but it never happens. He will always continue to come back, unless he has the intelligence to stay away. I am not calling you stupid, but uneducated. You tried to help your mom, but who tried to help you? Who told you that she needed professional help, and you needed a better home? You never had the chance to be taught that there was another place you could stay, like that stray dog."

I sat up and looked at Mr. Anderson. I understood what he was saying, even though it was a weird comparison. "I never did get that pat on my head, did I?"

"I guess not." He grinned a little, and I knew that therapy really wasn't that bad after all. I just could never admit to anybody that I ever went to a shrink.

I had a therapy session every day, and was starting to understand my past, and my present. It was really tough to go and listen to a stranger tell me what was wrong with my life. I thought of Steve, and what he had said to me so I would go there, and I pressed myself to talk about it. Soon, Mr. Anderson was no longer a stranger. Soon, he was almost like a friend. I liked him, despite the fact that he was a little dorky.

I didn't see Steve much. Mr. Anderson also gave Steve therapy, and even though patients' sessions were kept confidential, he would tell me that Steve wasn't doing that well. He had been doing drugs for so long in his life that totally depriving him of them now was driving him insane. Steve took them to escape from the world, like me. Steve talked to Mr. Anderson only to try to understand why he had to quit, because he knew he was uneducated. He had one thing that I didn't have then, hope. The one thing that stayed in Steve's heart the whole time was the will to have a future, and be able to walk out the front door of the rehab building, and know he would never do drugs again. He really didn't want to be in rehab, and that made the conversations tense, Mr. Anderson told me.

Every time I saw Steve he looked skinnier than before. His eyes were dark underneath, like he didn't sleep at all. He was scared of every sound that was made, like the bogey monster was behind every corner. He didn't talk that much, but when he did he mumbled and it was hard to understand what he said. He scared me.

It had been a month since I started rehab when I saw Steve for the last time. I was on my way to therapy while he was on his way back. "Hey, Steve." I waved, but he didn't respond. I went over and poked him, and he awoke from his world.

"Oh, hey Pete." He mumbled a little. "What's up?"

"I'm doing better, Steve. How about you?" He looked down the hall, going back to his own world.

"I can't take it anymore, man. I've had enough. I give up. I need something to get me through the day; and they won't give me anything. What am I supposed to do?"

I put my hand on his shoulder. It sank a little, like my hand weighed ten pounds. "Don't give up, Steve. You are the one who talked me into coming here, and I'm getting better. You have to, too. Come on, don't give up. You can make it, and after, we'll find us some girls."

He cracked a smile. I hadn't seen him smile since Eric and I succeeded at the hustling match. He seemed so incredibly depressed, and somehow I knew he wasn't going to make it through. I never had seen Steve like that before. He used to be such a hyper happy person, like Adam. Now, he was depressed, and not letting anyone in to help him. All I could do was hope.

We went on our ways, and I looked back at him as he continued down the hall. He seemed to be in one big nightmare, and no matter how much he pinched himself, he couldn't wake up. I just hoped Mr. Anderson could get through to him like he did me.

The day after I saw Steve, I was feeling better than expected. I knew I was going to leave that place soon. When I walked into Mr. Anderson's office like usual, he wasn't in there. I decided to sit and wait for him, but he didn't come.

After ten minutes, I left and went outside. It was warm and bright. I liked nature, though I never admitted it to anybody. There was a nice garden there, where I loved to go and sit, just staring at the birds in their cheerful moods. They never seemed to have any problems, and I would wonder what it would be like to have no worries.

I felt somebody sit on the bench beside me, and I turned to

see who it was. Mr. Anderson picked up some grass and started pulling it apart. He seemed upset about something. "Sorry I wasn't in my office."

"It's cool. I like it out here, it's nice." I looked at a squirrel who ran by and I thought how animals like these could live in the middle of the city.

"I have some bad news, Pete." I looked at him. He seemed young, sitting in the sun. His gray hair seemed to blend in with his brown, and his glasses weren't as visible in the position I was in.

"As long as you don't say I have to stay here for another month, I'll be fine. I don't know what I would do if you told me that." I smiled a little, but his expression didn't change, at all.

"It is worse than that. A boy hung himself last night, one of my patients. It was quite dramatic. It scared me a little, but I know there was nothing I could do for him. How I wish there was, but he was in his own world. No matter how hard he tried to leave, he was stuck there."

"Who was it?" I said after a while, but I really didn't want to know. My voice was just trying to break the tensional silence.

"It was Steve, Pete." Then he looked at me for the first time since he sat down. I could see it in his eyes that I might overreact. I just sat there though, not really stunned, but upset.

"I'm not surprised," I said bluntly. Mr. Anderson looked at me more intensely. "I saw him yesterday. Just yesterday; it seems now a year ago. He didn't look so good. I could tell he hadn't had any sleep and he was depressed beyond help. He was my best friend and I will miss him, but I am not surprised. Is that bad?"

"No, not at all." He dropped the grass that he had been shredding and picked up some more to tear the life out of. "I'm more than surprised at how well you took this, to tell you the truth. I know how good of friends you were, and it will be hard to cope. I just want you to know that if you ever feel in a state where you feel there is nothing else to do but die, seek help. It is your only way out. I knew he was bad off, but I didn't expect suicide. Maybe I should have spotted it."

"Oh, no you don't. It couldn't have been your fault; he had a bad life. Don't blame yourself, or else I might have to hit you again." He laughed, and I knew he understood perfectly.

"The funny thing is, he was always worried about you. Every day I would see him, and he would ask how you were; if you started talking to me yet, or if you were doing any better. He sounded like a big brother. He was not worried about himself, but you and the world around him. Soon his own world was tired of being neglected." He stared at the ground where he had dropped his last handful of shredded grass.

"He was my big brother. I mean, not literally, but sensibly. I will miss him, he was my best friend. I just don't understand why everyone I love either dies or leaves me." Mr. Anderson put his hand on my shoulder.

"Don't blame yourself either, Pete. People don't die because of you. You don't have some powerful disease that rubs off and acts as poison to the people you love. None of this is your fault, and if you think it is, I will have to punch you instead." We laughed, and I knew then everything was going to be okay.

I left two weeks after the news. Mr. Anderson asked Ms. Belgy to find another therapist for me, just to help me out. He also told me to be careful, and keep my head up high (whatever that means). I was so happy to leave, but I had to stop and wish Steve was coming with, too.

Everybody was happy to see me, but they were all depressed over Steve. He was quite popular because he was so understanding and loveable. We had a ceremony in his honor, something we never did for Eric. I asked Ms. B why we never did anything for Eric but have a moment of silence. She said it was because people were more scared of him than anything else. Steve was liked, and there needed to be something done in his honor. He died trying to become a better person, but could not make it.

I had tried so many times to block out Steve's death. No matter how hard I persisted, the images I had, just stayed in my mind and played like a TV show. After the ceremony, I went up to my room, lay down on my bed, and cried like a baby. I had been strong for too long and I just needed to let it all out. It surprised me that I felt so much better after.

After a couple of days of settling back in, Ms. B called me into her office again. Of course it scared me; last time I had to go in there I was sent to a place where my best friend died. I went in and sat, though. My knees were a little shaky because I thought bad news was ahead.

"I wanted to tell you how happy I am that you are back, and well. You won't have to leave, but will have to be straight until the day you die, or else more trouble could happen. Okay?" She smiled, and I nodded. Ms. B wasn't mad at me anymore, which thrilled me.

"I know that you will probably not be too happy about this other thing that I have to tell you, but I had to do it. The social services said it was his right to know what was going on with his son." I knew the next thing that was to come out of her mouth and I really didn't want to hear it. "I got in touch with your father. His name is Chris Odwick. He lives in Virginia. He will be here in two days."

"How could you? Why? Don't you realize I don't ever want to see him? Why should I see him; he hasn't even bothered seeing me in 17 years!" I was standing up, practically jumping up and down. How could she do that to me? "Why, Ms. B? Do you want me to go back into drugs again or something?"

"Oh my God, Pete, of course not! He has to see you, you have to see him. He is your father, he wants to see you, anyway. Give him one chance, just one. He was really young and scared when you were born. Just see him once, and then I will never make you see him again."

I sat back down. I thought I was going to pass out. See my father? That idea was beyond insanity. Why would he want to see me? After all that time, after all I went through, why would he want to see me then? "It will be my birthday when you say he is supposed to show."

"I know," she said quietly. I think she was glad I sat back down. "He knows, too." Great, he knows my birthday, too. That thrilled me.

"Are you sure I should do this?" I looked into Ms. B's eyes. I needed some guidance through this; I didn't know what to do. That was my runaway father we were talking about.

"Yes, I do."

"Fine." I left, and walked to my room to soak all of it in. I was to see my father in two days, on my seventeenth birthday. I was to see the father I had never seen before, on my birthday, and not my mom, Eric, Adam, Suzy, or Steve. I had lost a lot of people, but I didn't know if I wanted to gain one, especially that creep.

Chapter 9

I sat in the chair uneasily. The past two days had gone by so slowly that I thought this day would never come. The day was pretty special for me. I was so happy to admit that I was straight, and even happier to receive gifts. The kids didn't give me much, but who could blame them? Only one boy in the whole orphanage actually had a job; the others only had their allowance money, which they needed for more important things. I did have the honor of opening the wrapping paper to a few CDs from some people, a CD carrier from Ms. Belgy, and school supplies from Ms. Sameson (ha, ha).

It was fun walking into the cafeteria and seeing the big banner that said "Happy Seventeenth Birthday, Pete Saleton." Everybody came up to greet me, and I was happy to see Ms. Sameson; I hadn't seen her for a while. I still felt a little gloomy, though, without all the other people I loved to be there with me. And, I was scared for the moment when I would meet *him.*

Ms. B sat me down in the front hall so I could see him when he walked in. So, I just sat there, fidgeting. He was already twenty minutes late and another twenty, I would have left. Some of my friends would pass by and smile, but they had no idea what it was like. They were all jealous that I was able to hitch a ride out of there, but I didn't want a ride with him.

Feelings flooded back to me that day. I hadn't missed them much, and then I wished them gone. I was scared, for nothing, but yet, something. It was hard sitting there, waiting. I wished badly for some drug, but I couldn't. After all that hard work to rid myself of it, I wanted it again. I thought of Steve then, and how he didn't want to be addicted. Then I thought of Eric. I wished Suzy was there supporting me, but I knew she would never come back, and I felt lonely. Everyone I loved was gone and I was lonely.

I did not want to meet him. He killed my mom and made me suffer. He should just rot in hell. Then I thought of my dream. My one dream, to be better than my parents. How could I do that on my own? What if this guy, Chris Odwick, had money. He could pay for college. I didn't have to live with him that long, anyway. Only a year, then I was out of there. At least I hoped that.

"Pete, how are you doing? Are you hanging in there? He should be here any minute. Just wait a little longer." I looked at Ms. B. She sure was nice, almost like a mother. I forced myself to smile at her, in recognition that I was fine. She left so that I could be by myself.

I went back into my world and one question popped into my head. Why was this happening on my birthday? I only had one seventeenth birthday and he had to ruin it. I could have been out at a party, going for a drive, doing something with my friends, anything instead of sitting there, waiting. Why did he have to come on my birthday?

Then I heard it, the knock. I jumped a little when it sounded, and then settled back down. I was not about to answer it; I would just end up slamming the door in his face. Ms. B did the honors for me, and I just sat there until she moved out of the way for me to see him.

"Hello, Mr. Odwick. It is nice to meet you. Please come in." Ms. B stepped out of the way as a tall, slender man walked in. His deep rumbly voice said thank you, and it scared me a little. "Pete is right over there."

I wished she hadn't pointed at me. I wished I could have just run away and forgot about ever meeting him. It didn't happen that way; he walked up to me instead. He stood five feet away, as if he came too close he would catch some horrible disease from me. He scared me as he towered over me, maybe six and a half feet from the ground.

I stood, to at least try to match his eye level. It was no use, he was a foot taller than me, if not more. We just stood there staring at each other, neither saying a word. What was there to say? Nice to meet you, dad? My heart beat incredibly loud and I wondered if his did the same.

He looked so young, too young. He was not my father. No gray hair, just short black curly hair, like mine. His eyes were coal black, and empty, they were so empty... His rough beard made him look like a lumber jack. He was not my father.

I didn't think either of us was going to say anything. He looked almost as surprised as me. He just kept staring at me, looking up and down. His eyes wandered from mine, to my toes, to my hair. He looked almost, proud? But why? How could a father who never even met his son be proud of him?

His voice interrupted the silence. "I, um, brought you something for, um, your birthday." He stuttered at every word and I wondered if he was as nervous as I was. He handed me a square box wrapped in blue paper and tied in a purple bow. The first present from my, dad. "You can open it if you want to." He noticed my hesitation.

I didn't want to open it. I wanted to throw it at him. "No, not really." I was very blunt. I hated that man. That Chris Odwick, that man who handed me a present tied in a bow. I wondered if it was a bomb. He nodded his head, almost in understanding. How could someone understand you if they didn't even know you?

"I'm really happy to meet you, Pete. I am sorry I haven't until now." He gave me a slight grin and I punched him right in the face. It felt good to finally hit the man who ruined my mom's life. He deserved to rot in hell and he was lucky that all I did was hit him.

He fell to the ground when I hit him in the nose. He held it with one hand, and then looked at the blood. Ms. B, who was standing by the stairs the whole time, ran over to him to make sure he was okay. I took one last look at the man who killed my mom, threw his present at him, and ran back to my room.

I stood beside my window and stared at the wall next door. I had made friends with that wall over the time I had spent at the orphanage. I knew every brick as well as I knew all of my fingers.

When I stared at the wall, I didn't have to think about the world downstairs, the world that included my father. I was glad I had hit him, but I knew he was my only chance out of there. It didn't matter then, everyone I loved either was dead or gone forever. I just wanted to make sure the next person that I would meet wouldn't become too close.

I had learned to hate the world in six months. Everything I thought good, turned bad. Everyone I loved, went away. Everywhere I turned, there was another evil being done. I didn't want to forgive the world yet, or the people in it. Even the person lying on the ground at the bottom of the stairs. He didn't deserve forgiveness, for if he never messed around with my mom, none of this would have happened. It wouldn't have happened because I wouldn't have been there for it to happen.

A knock at my door disrupted my thoughts, but I did not go to answer it. The footsteps that came closer did not sound like Ms. B, but I did not turn to see who it was. I knew it was him and I didn't want to talk to him; I just wanted him to leave. He could not read inside my head and came to stand beside the window with me.

"I know you must hate me; I ruined both your life, and your mom's. I just hope someday you can somehow forgive me." He stared at me, but I kept looking out the window.

"How? How am I supposed to forgive you? You ruined my mom, she's dead now. Do you know that? Did you know she committed suicide? Why did you run away from her? You killed my mom, and my life." My voice stayed at one level, surprisingly. I still wonder that I didn't push that creep out the window and watch him plummet to his death.

"I was only seventeen when she became pregnant; I didn't know what was going to happen. I did not want to raise a family while still in high school. I was scared, so I ran. I know now that was the worst thing I could have done, but then I was too young to know any different. I should have come back when I grew up, but I didn't. I thought it would be better if I just left your mom alone. I thought her parents would support her; they had a lot of money. I did not know they would kick her out. All I can do now is apologize. Nothing else can be done." He drifted off into a whisper.

"Why did you come back? I was doing just fine without you." Meeting him was hard, I didn't want to understand where he was coming from. I didn't want to know why he left.

"That is not what I heard. Ms. B called me when you were in rehab. Pete, I came back to help you out. You need somebody to watch you and take care of you. Obviously, you weren't doing well on your own. Your life has been hard, you need a break, and I'm here to give it to you. I came back to take you home." He went to touch my arm, but I quickly backed away.

"Don't touch me," I warned. "I don't need your help. There is nothing you can do but make me mad." I gave him a hard look, but he just stood there with sympathy in his eyes. How could he give me sympathy? He was the pathetic one.

"There is something I can do; take you away from the city. You need to go out into the country and live in a real house, and start your life anew. Pete, I can give you a future." He stood there looking at me, and I went and sat on the bed. I put my head in my hands and stared at the floor. I couldn't believe that a dad who I never met before came on my seventeenth birthday to offer me a future. How could he offer such a big present?

There was silence in the room and all I wanted him to do was leave. He wanted me to go back and live with him, like father and son? No, I thought. No, I couldn't. He was the man I most despised.

"Pete, I know this is hard for you, but..." I interrupted him.

"How do you know this is hard? This never happened to you! Your family is still alive. Your dad didn't leave you and never make any contact. So, how do you know?" He walked over and sat against the wall that faced my bed.

"You're right, I don't know how this feels. I can only imagine it must be hell. You're right, I had a normal life with a normal family. But you're wrong about the living family part. My parents died in a plane crash a year ago. My only living relative is you, my son."

I lifted my head and stared at him. "How can you say that? Call me your son, you can't. If I was your son, you would have been there to watch me grow up. You would have been there on my first day of school. You would have been there when I needed a father, but you weren't!" I rolled over to the other side of the bed and ran out of the room.

I ran down the stairs and turned the corner, heading to a back door. There lay a present, the present he brought me. I picked it up and threw it at the wall. It busted, and when the box landed, something rolled out. I went over to see what it was. A baseball lay in the middle of the hallway. I knelt down and picked it up. Then tears came, tears that I couldn't hold back.

I sat there in the middle of the hallway and stared at that baseball, the baseball that Chris Odwick brought me for my birthday. Chris Odwick came all the way from Virginia to give me a baseball, a baseball that he meant to give me when I was five years old. Chris Odwick, a dad who ran away from his family from fright. I sat there and stared at that baseball, and let the tears come. I had nothing to be ashamed of, crying was only human.

I felt a hand on my shoulder but I did not look up. "I thought you might like that." I did not respond, but just kept staring at the ball that my father gave me. A ball that was stitched like he wanted us to be.

He sat beside me, and stared at the ball, too. I wondered what he was thinking. "I never was here to give you a ball and glove, and send you off to little leaguers. I wish I was, I wish more than you will ever know."

I then realized where he was coming from. I didn't want to, I didn't want to understand him, or like him. But then, as I held that baseball, I yearned for the father I never had. I remembered when I used to stare at the stars and wonder what he was like; and now he was sitting there beside me. He was the replica of my imaginings.

"I know it wasn't your fault." I was still crying, but not making any noise. That was the first time that I didn't kick myself for crying like a wimp. "I also know that I do need help."

He put his hand on my shoulder, and out of the corner of my eye I could see a tear roll down his face. He smiled, though. "Thank you. Thank you for understanding."

I left the orphanage the next day and went on a plane for my first time. My dad reassured me during the whole flight, for I was terrified of going that high up into the sky. It was weird having a total stranger as a father, but that soon changed.

"Were your parents nice?" I stared out the small window and looked at the fields below us. He looked straight ahead as he answered the question.

"Yeah, real nice. I miss them, but I'm glad that I had them. When they died, that is when I realized what you didn't have. I tried to find you, but I'm sorry to say that I couldn't. When I called your mom's house, her parents refused to admit they even had a daughter. I can't believe that, even to this day. They used to baby her so much, and then they just abandoned her when she needed them most."

I looked at him; his eyes were almost as hard as mine. "If I learned anything at rehab, it was that people can be cruel. Sometimes it is not their fault, though."

He looked at me in understanding. "Yeah, that is true, isn't it?"

I smiled a little. "What my mom's parents did was wrong, but sometimes I try to think about it through their eyes. They lived in high society, and they didn't need her actions to bring them down. I try not to blame anybody about what happened; it is hard. I think the person I blamed the most was you."

He did not turn away, he did not flinch, he knew why I thought that. "I blame myself, too. That night should never have happened. It was wrong of me, but she didn't just sit there and not do anything. What did she tell you happened?"

I did not want to talk about my mom to him, I knew she wouldn't like that. But I knew he needed to know. "She never talked about it much. All she ever said was that men have too many hormones."

He laughed. "Yeah, she's right about that. But you need to know why this happened, Pete." He grew silent, trying to collect all of his thoughts. "We went to the same school, your mom and I. I was a senior and the captain of the football team. I was pretty popular and could catch any girl I wanted. I knew it, too. That is what got me into trouble. There was a really big party that one of my friends threw. Almost everyone in school was there, including your mom. Both of us were drunk, but it was my knowing that I could have any girl I wanted that caused it. She was just the pick of the draw."

I looked out the window. "I never wanted to know what happened. I just wanted to leave those events in the past."

"But you can't, Pete. You need to know why you are here. You need to know what can happen if you're not careful." I never liked lectures on sex, so I left to go to the "bathroom." When I sat back down, he said nothing. I was the one who started it.

"I'm sorry," I apologized. "I never had a father to talk to me about that before. I know about it all, don't worry. They teach you in school." We both laughed, and our friendship began. I never wanted to become friends with him before, but now I'm glad we did.

After our little "giggle," we sat in silence for a while. I still had unanswered questions, so I asked one more out of the blue. "Why did you come when Ms. B called? Why do you want me back after all of this time?"

He looked over at me and stared me in the eyes. "I told you I tried to find you, I wanted to have my son, like a family. That was a year ago, and the day Ms. B called me was the same day I had convinced myself you were not to be found. I was so happy she called me, I dropped everything and flew out to meet you."

"No regrets." I stared at the seat in front of me.

"None at all." He touched my hand when he spoke, and I looked back into his eyes. I knew then that this was my father, and friend.

Driving up his driveway was an adventure. His house was humongous. When he'd pulled up, I leaned against the car and stared at it.

"Nice, isn't it?"

I turned to him. "How can you afford a place like this?" He laughed and picked my bag up.

"Years of hard work." I followed him inside. "Let me show you your new room." He led me up a tremendously long staircase. I could not believe the room he took me in. It had a queen-sized bed, a beautiful dresser, and a desk. The best thing was a large window with a view of mountains. "I hope you like it," he said as he set my bag down.

I walked over to the window and stared at the scenery. I remembered my wish to look at something other than a brick wall. I couldn't believe it was true. "Yeah, I love it." He laughed a little. I knew then that it wasn't going to be too bad.

I stared out that window a lot when I moved in with my dad. Once I even saw a groundhog. It looked a lot like Mr. Pandle. But just staring out a window wasn't me. I had to be outside, feeling the air.

So, now I sit outside a lot and stare at the stars, wondering about my life and its future. I often think about my mom, Adam, Suzy, Eric, and Steve. I imagine them knowing my dream of finishing high school and going on to college to study law, and maybe even becoming a partner at my dad's law firm. Someday I could even be a father, a father who will be there to watch his children grow up into fine people. A father who will always be there for them, no matter what may happen.

Most of all, when I stare up at those stars at night, I look at just one star, and imagine that some other teenager is looking at the same exact star. He or she might be so scared and worried about this life. So I wish on that star that all their hopes and dreams will come true.

Collected Stories

Anonymous stories collected by Youth Voices

Story 1, Reflections and Consequences

There was a family of four - two boys, one little girl, and their mom - that lived in a small town. The father lived in another state after a shaky divorce and remarried with five children. The two younger children, Steven and Lori, went to a local grade school and the oldest boy, Chris, attended high school. They were an average small-town family.

One late night in the middle of winter, Chris came home to his mother, brother and little sister, drunk and out of control. He wanted the keys to his mother's car. His mother, of course, said no, and attempted to end the conversation at that, but Chris was drunk and ready to argue.

He screamed at his mother, attempting to win the fight and take the car, but she refused as the two younger children, Steven and Lori, stood by watching the verbal battle. Chris became so enraged he retrieved one of the loaded shotguns from the cabinet between the couch and the closet door. He continued to threaten his mother with this stronger force. There Chris stood with a gun pointed at the head of the sobbing woman while his brother and sister stood by crying out in horror. He asked her once more - but all she could do was cry... and a shot was fired.

A pool of blood surrounded a body lying limp on the floor. Then there was another shot. A second body fell. Chris fled the house, realizing the biggest mistake of his life. Steven lay sprawled across the floor with shock on his face. His mother lay next to him, her tears still warm.

Lori sat in the warm corner of the room in fear - she had witnessed the entire incident. She had seen her brother pull a gun on her mother. In a desperate attempt to spare his mother's life, Steven had jumped in front of his mother, catching the shot in the chest. Then she saw her mother shot and fall dead beside him...

Chris eventually turned himself in to the local police later that night, admitting to his crime. Before he left his house, he had brought Lori to a neighbor's house, not informing them of anything.

Lori, after a long and painful experience, went to live with her great grandmother in another state. Chris was convicted as a juvenile and remained in jail only until he turned 18 years old. Then he was released.

Story 2, Dumbfounded

Based on a true story, I will share the effects of alcohol seen in my life. Thought to be a cool thing to do, a bunch of students threw a party and invited me when I was a freshman. I went to this party with the exact intent to never do any drugs or alcohol and that was the way it was going to be. Well, at the party I kept that promise to myself and even though I was offered different brain killing substances, I stood my ground and just said no. I was so against drugs and alcohol that I would tell people that I knew used them that it was not healthy and definitely not safe but they proceeded on with their foolish ways. The sad part about it is that the person that I stressed it upon the most, well, she got pregnant and has a baby, and now is married at a very young age.

Wouldn't you know, there was another party that I was invited to and I went to this one too because I thought I would have a good time just hanging out with people. When I got to the party there were a lot of people there and amongst them all were my usual friends that I knew would be there drinking alcohol and I was okay with that. I like people and I don't judge people by their appearance, personality or anything along that line. I like to get to know everyone, and each person is different from you or I but that shouldn't leave you any room for being judgmental. Everyone has problems whether it is drinking, drugs, or just personal issues but you shouldn't dislike them for it. Would you want them to think that of you?

As the party proceeded I noticed that there was a group of

people huddled around each other, laughing at someone on the ground, so I went to investigate. To my surprise, I saw one of my very close companions that I thought had also promised that he would never drink, passed out from too much alcohol consumption. I was absolutely astonished; I had no clue that he was involved in these ludicrous activities. At that moment I though I was the only one that didn't do it.

I have built up a hatred for alcohol and/or drugs; the reason being is that I have seen what these substances can do. When I was six years of age, I heard a knock on my front door in the middle of the night that drew my parents out of bed. They regretted forever having to open the door because it was the police bringing the news of my 18-year-old brother's death, which had been caused by an OUI. With this having happened to me so young, it was, in a way, a wake-up call to drugs. To see everyday people drinking and having a good time, I'm always there worrying that someday one of them, my friends, will end up in the same place as my brother. This is why I need to watch after people and hopefully help them to realize the damage that alcohol and drugs have on your body and on everyone around you, both mentally and physically.

Story 3, Supernova

Hard to imagine that only two days ago my mother and I were screaming at each other. Hard to imagine that just yesterday Joe told me he was coming to pick me up to go to Randy Heatman's "jamming party." Hard to imagine that one mess up in the master plan could result in me sitting in the waiting room at the hospital, staring at a soda machine, trying to tell myself that neither one of these people in my life were going to die. It is hard to imagine that this wasn't just another bad dream.

My mother and I never did get along. She always screamed at me about one thing or another, whether it was about my long hair, or about my smoking habit, or even the friends I have, of which she doesn't approve. I'm just a normal teenage boy that doesn't get along with his parents, and who might have thoughts of them dying from a dramatic event so they cannot scream anymore. It's hard to imagine that one little thought such as that would ever come true.

No matter how much I resented her, or how much I hated wasting my time by sitting still while the rest of the world kept turning, I still found myself waiting in that room for some positive word from the doctor. My father kept pacing back and forth, and sometimes he would sit, sigh, and then continue his never-ending walk. I felt like smacking him. A person's sickness does not make the event of a marathon.

I could feel her eyes staring at me. Kelly, my sister, hadn't taken her glare off me since she picked me up from home. WE hadn't said a word since she told me about the accident, yet I knew she blamed it on me. Who wouldn't?

We had waited there for two hours before the first sign of a doctor was evident. She walked in, sat, and without saying a word, we knew.

"Things just didn't go as well as we suspected in surgery, and her internal bleeding was so severe, we just... I mean we couldn't... I mean, sorry."

Sorry? Is that what they always say when they tell a family that they no longer have a mother, a wife, a family member? Just I'm sorry, nothing else? They couldn't stop the bleeding, she was in bad shape, the doc said. Why? How?

I stood up and walked down the hall to see Joe. The sounds of my sister's cries, and my father's sighs, were unbearable. Imagine someone you once resented, but now loved, dead. Imagine wishing you weren't such a jerk, and hoping that they would know how you really felt.

Joe wasn't in that good of condition, but he would live. He was fine, and didn't know a thing that had happened. I stood in the doorway of his room and looked at him asleep on his little hospital bed, with a few bandages here and there, and not a sign of worry in his brain.

It was just yesterday he told me about the party. Just yesterday he told me that it was something that couldn't be missed. How stupid I was to believe him! If I had just stayed home for once, and ate dinner with my family like my mom asked, none of this would be true.

"Let's go," Joe had said, welcoming himself into my home. We got in his little Toyota and sped out of my neighborhood. I could already see the fight in my head that I was going to have with my mother when I would return. She would yell at me for being irresponsible, or too wild, or some crud like that.

Half the school showed for Randy Heatman's party. Everything that people said it was going to be, it was, and everything they couldn't imagine, it was. Loud music, a big bonfire, and all the beer one would want was there. A guy from Mexico was even here to visit. Everyone had a great time. By one o'clock, though, it died down. Most people left, but a great part of the people had crashed in Randy's basement. A few of us stayed a little later, drinking more and smoking some. By three o'clock, Randy was going around screaming at the people who hadn't left yet, and at the people who left a big mess. His parents were coming home the next day, and they didn't exactly know about the festivities.

Joe was smashed, but ready to leave at three-thirty. I wasn't so enthusiastic about getting in his car as he was. Driving made me sick, especially when I had beer and grass mixed in my stomach. He shrugged when I told him I thought I was just going to crash the night at Randy's. I asked him to do the same, so I could have a ride in a few hours, and so he wouldn't kill the whole world with his insane driving.

Joe was not a good driver to begin with. He's half blind, but refuses to wear his glasses, so he doesn't realize something is there until he is right there close to it. He slams on the breaks pretty hard, too. When he's on something, it's even worse. I've ridden with him before when he was like that, and it isn't fun. He swerves, and can't see things. He even sees things that aren't there.

Yet, no matter what I would say, he was going home, and there wasn't a thing I could do about it. That is why I didn't try as hard as I should have, I knew it was hopeless. I was asleep before he left.

One of my friends gave me a ride home at eight in the morning, an hour I didn't know even existed on Saturdays. Randy was still mad, and he let me know it before I left. He was rushing to have everything clean before noon.

No one was at my house when I got home. Joy overtook me before curiosity. For once, I wasn't going to be screamed at for having a little fun. I would also be able to sleep in peace. Before I could go to bed, though, the phone rang.

It was Judy, Joe's girlfriend. She had this pathetic sound in her voice, and it sounded like she had been crying.

"Joe is in the hospital," she told me. "He was in an accident earlier this morning. I just thought I should tell you."

I stood still for a while. Joe was insane, but he was also invincible.

"Is..." I couldn't talk too well. "He's okay, right?"

"We don't know yet. the doctors are still working on him. I gotta go, but come down if you can." She hung up, but I gripped harder to the phone.

Joe was in the hospital. My best friend was in the hospital. While I hung up the phone, I heard my sister walk in. I turned around to see her crying. Nothing seemed real.

"Come on, we got to go to the hospital," she said.

"I know, but how did you find out?" She stared at me for awhile.

"About Joe," I tried to unclog her memory. "How did you find out about Joe?"

"Mom's in the hospital, you idiot," she screamed. "Some idiot kid was driving drunk, and slammed right into her car."

Those words kept ringing in my ear. That idiot was my best friend. My best friend hit my mother, and killed her.

How could such a thing happen? My mother got a phone call from one of her friends. They were stuck on the side of the road from a drive back from North Carolina, and she was going out to help them. At four o'clock in the morning, my best friend hit my mother in a head-on collision at sixty miles per hour. She died, and he lies there in a bed without a worry.

Story 4, Close Call

It was pretty late by the time my mom, dad and I had gotten back from a friend's wedding. My brother had decided to stay home and have some friends over. As we walked in, we saw a note on the counter saying that my brother, Joey, was tired and decided to go to bed for the night.

Since he is older, we thought that this was very unusual. My dad went up to check on him. I had to go change out of my dress, so I was across the hall from Joey's room. After changing, I walked into my brother's room to find my dad trying to wake him up. He didn't move.

"Joey, wake up!" said Dad over and over, every time his voice got a little louder until he found himself hollering at Joey.

He still didn't move, but we made sure that he was breathing. The room reeked of alcohol and vomit. Dad told me to tell mom to call 911. Mom didn't know what was happening, then she became hysterical. We all were. She could barely talk on the phone as she shuddered and shook. We were all horrified and didn't know what was going to happen. I found it hard to talk or even move. I was jittering a lot. I felt a big pit in my stomach and it made me cringe. I thought I was going to throw up.

Finally, the ambulance showed up after what seemed like forever. One medic said that Joey could have died if he had thrown up while lying on his back. He would have choked to death on his own vomit. His blood alcohol level was .25, or something like that. The doctor said it was extremely high. It's a miracle he survived that night.

I don't think it's possible to imagine the fright and anxiety that people go through in situations like that, unless you've been through a similar one. It was the most frightening experience of my life.

Story 5, Hallucination

It was less than a half a week before it was time to go on our family vacation to Tennessee. I was sitting down in my mom's comfortable chair, getting ready to watch my favorite show, The Drew Carey Show. I couldn't wait to see it. It was suppose to be a new episode. I sat in the chair waiting for the show to begin, the phone rang. RING, RING, RING! At this point I thought nothing of the phone call. I just wanted to watch the show. So ignorant me, I let my mom pick it up because it was probably for her anyway. I thought it was one of my aunts or uncles, because of the reaction my mom had when the person answered. I still didn't care if it was one of my family members I don't get to talk to hardly at all. I just wanted to watch the show and laugh at all the stupid things. After the show was over, I got up and headed up stairs to go to bed. And at that moment my mom was getting off the phone.

"Who was that?" I asked curiously.

"That was Aunt Clare. She said that Uncle George is in the hospital." Mom didn't sound too happy about it, either.

"Why is he in the hospital?" I asked awkwardly.

"Well, he got very drunk last night and got alcohol poisoning. They said he might not make it until the end of the week." My mouth dropped open. Uncle George was my most favorite uncle out of them all. I almost lost it and started crying right there.

"We need to go see him sometime in the next few days."

I didn't know what to say. I was speechless. I never for my life thought that Uncle George would drink that much. After a couple of minutes I went to my room and tried to go to sleep. It was hard, but I did it. When I woke up the next morning, I tried to get rid of the idea that Uncle George would do something like that. Just after breakfast my mom said that after she got off work we were going to go to see Uncle George.

The pain of going to see my uncle stabbed me in the back all day. I didn't want to see my uncle before he was going to die. I really did, but I knew that I would feel weird. I didn't know how to handle it. All day I imagined what my uncle would look like when we got there. I envisioned him with a tube shoved down his throat, a tube stuck up his nose, three needles injected in both arms, and in a recovering room where you can't touch him.

When my mom returned from work she told my brother and I to get our stuff together and put it in the car, because she wanted to get there before dark. So, in our slow way we went up the stairs and threw some clothes together and some stuff to do, walked down stairs to the car, and got in. The ride was stone quiet. I was afraid to say anything to hurt my mom's feelings. I don't know what I would have said, but I know I would have said something wrong.

When we arrived at my aunt's house she greeted us with a happy face; even though she was crying inside, she looked wonderful on the outside. For the rest of the night I ate junk food and played my Gameboy. My mom and her sister talked about my uncle's problem with booze. I never knew he had a drinking problem. It felt weird not knowing that until then.

The next day, at my aunt's house, I woke up about ten o'clock and went to go take a shower. I was walking for the bathroom door and my mom forcefully said, "We have to leave now and go see Uncle George, since he is up RIGHT NOW. You can take a shower when you get back."

I stopped, looked at her, and gave her a begrudging look.

We reached the hospital at about eleven o'clock. When we entered the waiting room my mom said, "You guys stay here and wait for me to come out and get you. I want to talk to him alone for a minute."

We waited for a good half an hour. When she did come out, she was holding her feelings in and trying not to cry. I felt bad for her. Then I thought he might have died, which wouldn't have been cool.

"Come on guys, let's go see him." She managed to say, looking terrified.

"What's wrong mom?" I asked, horrified.

"He is so bad," she swallowed hard, "he's hallucinating. And... well, he can't remember a lot of people."

My stomach did a ten-eighty on me and slit itself open. As I walked closer to the door I became scared, very scared.

When we entered the room he was sitting up in his bed

looking at the ceiling with an awkward look on his face. When he noticed we were there, he glanced at us and said, "What the hell is dat damn dog doin' runnin' on the ceiling?"

We walked all the way in and looked at what he was looking at.

"There isn't anything there, George," my mom replied.

He wasn't listening. He wasn't there.

Story 6, Unwanted Memories

I have never understood the reason for alcohol, and never will. I will never be able to see drinking as fun, or something to loosen you up so you can be cool and hang with friends. I feel this way because alcohol was a huge part of my childhood, the huge part I would like to forget.

I can remember the long nights where I would wait for my stepmother to start something. When she drank, the only thing she wanted to do was fight. I could always tell when she got mad because she would have that look in her eye. It cut through me. I would always turn away and leave, wanting to cry.

With that look, I knew that she was going to blow up at any minute, and I didn't want to be there when she did. I would hear her yelling at first, then the doors would slam. It seemed like a routine that my father always fell for. After her blowout, she would be calm and it would seem like nothing had ever happened. Until night came, then her anger would spread like wildfire again.

The thing I remember the most was the yelling in the night. It would always wake me up. Once I remember running out of bed and into the hall and seeing my father lying on the floor. He had a shocked look on his face, and a streak of fear in his eyes. My stepmother was standing above him with a phone wire that was wrapped around his neck. She saw me and dropped it. That night my father had charges brought against him from my stepmother, and I said nothing. Their marriage lasted for eighteen years. My father was blamed for being the bad guy all those years.

My stepmother never really stopped drinking after my father and her split up, but the pain her children endured and the continuous grief my father suffered were gone.

My stepmother and father have now been divorced for about six years, and I live with my father. I see her from time to time. The cold hated things she did will stay in my mind forever. I will never be close to her.

Story 7, Alcoholism

Alcoholism has touched my life in various ways. Throughout my life my mother has always been a heavy drinker. My dad has always been home with us and my mom has always seemed to miss out on so much. After my parents got divorced I started realizing something wasn't right in my mother's life: my life also.

As I got into my teenage years, I realized really how much my mom missed out on. I would ask her to come to concerts and she'd forget. I would ask her to baseball games, and soccer games, and school outings, and still she'd forget. On occasion my mom would show up, late and intoxicated. It didn't bother me at the time. I had never thought of my mom being controlled by a substance. Especially alcohol. I didn't even know what alcoholism was.

My dad would try and explain as I got older and started figuring something wasn't right. He told me my mother had a disease that was no longer in her control. She needed help. I would yell at my dad and tell him that wasn't the truth, that he had no idea what he was talking about. I would go in my room and cry for hours.

My brothers and I started going to counseling. There, many questions were asked. My brothers and I were being pushed to speak of something we had not yet accepted. It hurt to hear someone telling us how our mother was, and how her "disease" would only get worse. As a child, one does not want to hear that about their mom. I was still close with my mom. When I was around her I paid more attention to what she was doing. I had always wondered why she'd fall asleep at the dining table and I couldn't wake her up. I'd watch empty bottle after empty bottle get tossed in the recycling bin. Clueless, I'd forget about it and try to brush it off.

Eventually I started to accept what was going on. I had a hard time dealing with this, but I knew it had to be dealt with. I talked to people I was comfortable around about my family's problem and listened to all the feedback I got. I have gotten so much support in dealing with this issue.

Alcoholism continues to be a problem to me, but now I can better understand it. I still can't or won't talk to my mom about the issue, but I pray that one day we will both be strong enough to sit down and talk about it. My mom is very important to me and I don't want to lose her to alcoholism.

Story 8, Sliding Down the Slope of Alcoholism

I have a cousin who is and was a very nice person. He married a woman we will call Julie. They were very happy together at first. I can honestly say that I know they truly loved each other. They both had a child from a previous marriage, which made things a little harder for them. Although both children lived with the other parent, there were still small disputes on who was favored.

When they got married, I noticed that they both drank frequently, but I didn't think anything of it. Later on, I began to see something happening. I started visiting their house quite frequently when I turned eleven. Their daughter and I are the same age. I liked to visit.

My cousins, John and Julie, were not home very often because they worked a lot. They painted houses and got paid very well for it. The strange thing was, they didn't have much to show from it. I couldn't help but wonder where their money was going.

They were both very nice in the evenings, but in the mornings they were always grumpy and didn't feel good. I noticed that they started fighting a lot. They were also very testy with us. They had low tempers, constant headaches, and mood swings. Eventually, John stopped coming back when he said he would. He'd come home very late and make excuses about what he was up to. Keep in mind that all these nights he was drunk. That's how the problems started. Those problems persisted and became worse.

Eventually, he wouldn't let Julie out of the house, although each night he went out. When it got really late and Julie was drunk and depressed, she would call the bar where he was supposed to be, and each time he was not there. I would stay up with her while she cried and cried. All of this, the going out and constant drunkenness by my cousin, the long nights with Julie drunk and upset, lead to a shocking ending to their marriage.

All this made me feel terribly bad, but I thought it couldn't be that bad, could it? Oh how wrong I was. I slowly noticed that things were getting much worse. She would cook, clean, and try to continuously satisfy him. He was never pleased and always hollering. He got very angry one night when he came home late and Julie confronted him.

He said, "I was at my girlfriend's house."

He wasn't lying. He then told Julie that he had been at his girlfriend's house all along. In a drunken rage he raised a hand to her. She left him, and never came back. They still both abuse alcohol. Julie moved in with the first person that she thought had any compassion for her, and John moved to Florida. Still running away from his problems.

Story 9, The Effect

How has alcohol affected my life? If you think about it, there are many places where it has touched my life. Recently I was surprised to learn that a police chief stated that if alcohol wasn't a factor he could cut his police force in half. My grandmother died as an alcoholic before I even met her and there is this constant pressure from peers to get drunk as a "cool and fun" thing to do. During every week at least a few pit parties are busted in the area in which I live. When alcohol is abused it causes people to do things they may not normally do and I have witnessed this first hand.

I was in third grade when the following events happened, and surprisingly I remember them very well. (Well, when your life is in danger I guess things stick in your mind.) Across the street from my house lives a drunk who just about every day takes a walk to the local store and comes back with a bag full of booze. He would sit in his car, rain or shine, and stare at us, gulping down the beer, as we did any outside activity.

One summer day I was playing as any third grader would be, and he started to walk toward me. Then suddenly, with surprising speed he started running straight at me. Slightly stunned with this action, I could hear my parents' voices faintly as if they were an echo, although they were only about 300 feet away. Then reality dawned on me, and after taking a quick look at him and his determined drunken expression, I ran as fast as my little legs could carry me.

Later he circled the house with a large stone, trying to break in. Needless to say, the police were called and he was very drunk. Soon after, an ambulance took him away after he had passed out.

Story 10, From the Ukraine to the U.S.A.

My name is Amanda and I am going to write about alcohol and my experience. I am going to tell you a little story about what happened to me in the past. I am from the former Soviet Union. I lived in the Ukraine where you're supposed to be eighteen to drink alcohol, but in our country no one ever listens to anyone. As a result you are able to drink any time and at any age.

I was watching a lot of movies and I saw people drinking

alcohol in there. At school my friends kept telling me how they got drunk over the weekend, how cool it is, and how brave you are. One day my friend asked me if I wanted to go party with her, and I said yes. They bought some alcohol and we went to my friend's house. They asked me to try alcohol; they said it was very cool. I tried it, because I thought I will be cool like my friends. I got drunk and it was kind of scary, because I didn't know how it felt to be drunk.

I didn't stop, I kept partying with my friends all the time, and I thought that I was cool. Eventually I stopped because I kind of got sick of it. I forgot about alcohol for a while until I met a guy and he asked me out. He was drinking a lot, and when he was drinking he asked me if I wanted some. A couple times I said no, but he was asking me so many times, he and I started drinking together.

Alcohol affected me very badly. My grades at school became lower. I started to lie to my parents a lot. All the money that I had I spent on alcohol. I started eating more and I gained a lot of weight. It was very sad. I looked much older and my face changed a lot.

When my family found out that I was drinking alcohol they were very sad. At first they couldn't believe that I was drinking. Then they realized the truth and they were very upset.

When I asked my best friend to come drink with me, she said no. She tried to stop me from drinking, but I didn't listen to her. Because of this, I lost my friend.

The reason I stopped drinking was because I moved to the U.S.A. Here everything is different, and I am not able to drink if I am not twenty-one. Another reason was because my parents talked to me a lot about it, so I understood that it's very bad for me and I shouldn't do it.

Now my life is changed. I don't drink anymore and I am playing a lot of sports. I don't even think about alcohol anymore. I am happy!!!

Story 11, Lost Journal

I walked through my junior year in a cloud. I learned a lot but also messed up a lot. My guidance counselor came into school the first day and told us that this would be the most important year of high school. He was not kidding when he said that. I learned more that year than any other. Not only did I learn from teachers and friends, but I learned from experience.

Age seventeen wasn't the easiest of the teenage years. Not only was I going through huge changes in life, but I also needed to worry about colleges. Moreover, I needed to worry about what I was going to do with my life once I left this pit of a town. Consequently, the word stress couldn't even come close to what I experienced. For this reason, I went through a duration of my junior year in a liquor bottle.

I partied every weekend, smoked, drank, lied and lost respect for myself and from my mom. My getaway from school and life was alcohol. I loved it because when I was drunk, I didn't think about my problems. When I didn't have alcohol though, I punched things, was irritable and altogether unfriendly. I hated being like that. I secluded myself in my room when I was actually home, and when I wasn't home I was usually drinking. I chose the easy way out of the problems and the challenges that I faced.

I have always trusted my friends immensely; I have never had a reason not to trust them. That is, until one week when my journal went missing from my room. This was having my deepest thoughts invaded without my consent. I suspected one of my friends who had always expressed curiosity about my journal and what I wrote in it. I investigated for a week but I couldn't find anything. In fact, I even tore my room apart to look for it. Still nothing showed up, so my solution to that problem was to say "@$%# you!" to my friends, and to get drunk.

After my journal was stolen, I secluded myself from everyone but my best friend. My friends didn't understand why I didn't want to hang out. They made up their own excuses why I wasn't around. All my emotions and anger were building up and I couldn't find a way to relieve my frustration. My nerves were shot, I had outrage towards everyone. I was drowning myself in tears, and in my actions. By the end of the week I was mentally exhausted. I got high and couldn't control my heart rate.

My heart felt like it was trying to burst through my body. It felt like I was having a heart attack. I called my mom at eleven at night and told her that I needed to go to the hospital. On the way down to the hospital we had a long, long talk.

I told my mom everything that I had been doing behind her back for the past four months. My mom told me that I will make many mistakes in my life and that I would learn from this one. She also told me that she raised me in a way that I would have to learn from my mistakes on my own and she wasn't going to stop that learning process. She also comforted me in saying that I could talk to her about absolutely anything.

While sitting in the waiting room, I honestly thought that I was going to die. The doctor said that I was experiencing an anxiety attack. I was fortunate that it wasn't anything more serious than that. I did things that I am not very proud of and I thank God that I am still walking this earth.

After all of this happened, I stayed home for a while. I didn't want to be around anyone. I didn't want to talk to anyone. Also, I needed time to reflect on the previous months and what had happened to me. As a result, I grew to be a better person. I was very lucky, no punishment was put upon me by my mom. I had my own punishments: losing my respect, my dignity, and also my mom's trust. I am proud to say that I have regained my mother's trust and that I have been clean from drugs for seven months now.

I had to go through all of those hard times to make me realize that drugs are not the answer to any problem. Every step in life is a lesson, and everything happens for a reason. I believe there must be some reason why I lost that journal. I never found it, but I found myself. Losing it made me face what I was going through and not become that person I've always told myself I would never be. My lesson hit me hard, and man, did I learn.

Story 12, The Fair Incident

I got off the bus with Susie and went to NNP to pick up Betsy and Harry to go to the fair. Susie and I walked for quite a while before we finally arrived at Betsy and Harry's house.

We picked up Harry and Betsy and headed to the fair. We walked for about ten minutes and arrived at the fair. Nothing much was going on. We had walked around the midway a couple of times when Harry, Betsy and Larry needed a smoke. They walked out of the midway, and since I don't smoke I stood around and waited for them to get done puffin'.

About five minutes later, Larry showed up and I hung with him for quite a while; then we went and sat on a table that was there. Harry saw these guys, so he jumped in the car with them for unknown reasons. Then all of us went over to the car to see what was goin' down. There were two guys in the car, one of legal age and the other not.

We were just hangin' around, one of the guys in the car was checking out Susie, and then they hauled out the hard stuff: menthol snapps. They had two glasses that were full of lemonade and the menthol stuff.

One of them asked me, "You wanna drink?"

I said, "Sure."

I drank all of his; then the other guy gave me his - it was mixed a heck of a lot stronger, and I drank that too. Then they poured the menthol snapps into another glass STRAIGHT, and I downed it...

Later on, we were walking around the midway and I was having a major BUZZ going on and I said that I needed to sit down, so we went and sat down, so we went and sat at a table. I was giggling a real lot, I could see some major, major blurred vision.

Then someone said, "Adult, adult, keep cool!" and I was too drunk to keep cool.

Then I said, "Ha ha ha ha ha, I know you..."

We all got up, and we scrammed out of there... so we were walking down the midway... and I felt a little WOOOOOZY. I told Larry that I needed to run and go into the woods... where I leaned against a tree and fell asleep.

Then I just woke up to sounds: "There he is."

Larry and all those guys hauled me out of the woods and brought me out and put me in the back of someone's pick-up, and then that dude came and said,"Get him outta here." So they hauled me back off into the woods and leaned me against a huge tree.

Everyone left me except for Susie; she stayed with me, but that doesn't matter 'cause she should have got help. Next thing I knew, people were telling me to SHUT UP, and that I was annoying, and they were hitting me and punching me and kicking me when I was still drunk.

Then after a long time a van arrived, and they were asking where I was. Susie told me to climb up in the woods, because someone is looking for me, so I did 'cause I was drunk.

I didn't know then, but the people in the van came to my rescue. In the end they brought me to their house and called my dad.

This has been told to you as I experienced it.

Let this be a lesson, 'cause I learned mine from it.

Some Things To Remember Day To Day

Life\'lif\n.;pl.lives\'livz\. The time during which a person or thing is alive or exists.

Life is more than just a length of time you spend in existence, counting days until your death. Life is friends, family, knowledge, pain, anger, bliss, love, hate, tears, giving, sharing, midnight bike rides on the beach, falling down the stairs and laughing, falling up the stairs and laughing, hanging out at the corner store just because you have nothing else to do, helping someone who needs you, striving to do your best and managing to do your worst. Life doesn't have a simple definition or answer to every question that a soul could ever ask. Life doesn't give and life doesn't take. Life is something that happens unexpectedly when the world seems like it's falling on your head and you can't stop it. But at the same time, life is the most beautiful thing nature has to offer - the most precious gift almost no one treasures...

Do things that make you happy. Do things that challenge you and give you better knowledge and better skills. Love the things you have. Ask if you want something. Talk if you need something. Love children. They are the future to everything in this world. Be kind to them, teach them, and care for them. Laugh every once in a while - you will be suprised how good it really feels. Forget the insults, remember the compliments. Push for what you believe is right. Don't ever give up.

Remember that your childhood is a period in your life full of bad and good beginnings; the rest of your life is the time you spend trying to overcome those beginnings. In life's trials it might seem like the whole world is against you, but there are people out there that care for you and want you to succeed. They will help you if you ask them, they will hold your hand, if not physically, then mentally.

So we leave you with the best of thoughts - sometimes you feel like there is nothing left to live for, no meaning to life. But, when you feel that emptiness slip through your body, remember to look inside yourself, look at all the people that care for you, look at all the things you have and all the things you don't have.

Our advice to you is to dream: dream of a world of perfect happiness. Use your tears to float your happiness, use your happiness to float you dreams and hopes. Find your true inner self. Remember it all starts with you.

The authors have agreed to remain anonymous and have changed names and circumstances of any stories that are based on personal experience in order to represent in story form the essential themes that are repeated in many people's lives without referring to any persons living or dead.

Youth Voices

The Carrabec Youth Voices Task Force is a part of the Maine Youth Voices project developed by the Maine Office of Substance Abuse (DMHMRSAS) and funded by a federal grant from the Office of Juvenile Justice and Delinquency Prevention. The goal of the project is to actively involve youth in reducing underage drinking in their communities. The project is administered by AdCare Educational Institute.

Maine Youth Voices was designed to focus on underage drinking as a community issue for which youth can craft solutions. Youth have important insights into the issue, and their knowledge, creativity and enthusiasm should be considered a crucial resource in any community's efforts to reduce underage drinking. Youth and adults need opportunities to build positive relationships in order to work together. The media is an important resource that should be tapped to help build solutions.

The Carrabec Youth Voices is one of fifteen Maine Youth Voices groups. Carrabec High School is a regional high school located in North Anson, Maine, with an enrollment of approximately three hundred students. This particular group believes that it is their mission to increase awareness of the important issues and problems in the community as a whole, and to provide positive alternative choices for young people, as the more options people know that they have, the more freedom they feel to discover themselves. The solutions to such problems become more evident with such liberty.

The Carrabec Youth Voices would like to thank the U.S. Department of Justice, the Maine Department of Substance Abuse, The Office of Juvenile Justice and Delinquency Prevention, AdCare Educational Institute, and Polar Bear and Company for their support. In addition, we would like to thank the community, students, teachers and administration at Carrabec High School for contributing stories, time and encouragement to such an exciting project.

Task Force

"In September of 1999, Maine PBS began working with students at Carrabec High School in North Anson as they actively explored peer pressure and community norms and the impact these factors have on teenage drinking. This group of young people participated in the hands-on production of a Youth Voices television documentary and Public Service Announcement. The program ultimately won a national Parents Choice Silver Medal award. Maine PBS has had a wonderful experience working with young people who are searching for new ways to exercise their artistic talents to share their voices, and now their *One Dream.*" –Kimberly Lipp, Special Projects Manager, Maine PBS.

Polar Bear and Company wish to give a special thanks to the Youth Voices Task Force members who worked very hard on this project.

Design and Layout Team: Alex du Houx, Trey Gaw, Aaron Knight, Kyle Metivier, Kelly Rudman.

Press Release Team: Rachel Brown, Emily Dawes, Kelly Rudman, Kyle Sawyer.

Endorsements team: Megan Carbone, Alex du Houx.

The entire task force edited and collected the stories: Aja Brill, Rachel Brown, Megan Carbone, Emily Dawes, Kate Drummond, Alex du Houx, Trey Gaw, Aaron Knight, Melinda Knowles, Mollie McGlocklin, Kyle Metivier, Kelly Rudman, Kyle Sawyer, Josh Turner.

Adult coordinator: Kate Drummond.

Youth coordinators: Rachel Brown, Kyle Metivier.

The Carrabec Youth Voices Task Force with the Governor Angus S. King Jr.
Top row: Kate Drummond, Mollie McGlocklin, Kyle Metivier, Governor Angus King, Rachel Brown, Alex du Houx, Kyle Sawyer. *Bottom row:* Emily Dawes, Kelly Rudman, Megan Carbone, Melinda Knowles. photo © Ramona du Houx.

Bet Shoshannah Pecora currently resides in Hume, Virginia, a small town where she has lived her entire life. She wrote her book, *One Dream*, at the age of fifteen, and hopes to write and publish more works like it.

Besides writing, Bet Shoshannah spends her time playing her piano, violin, guitar, drums, and even sings in a choir. Living in a part of the country where horses are especially popular, she has taken up riding, and looks forward to owning some horses one day.

Bet Shoshannah wrote this book to inform teenagers her age about the harsh world. While doing this, she hopes to open some eyes that are currently shut, and maybe influence even one person from doing anything that would harm their life, or lives of others.